Special thanks to all those who helped with this project:
Chase Whiteside
Timm Derrickson
Leif Derrickson
Laura Register

I0548327

My wife, Julie, and son David

My Sisters
Elaine, Judy, Sam, Frankie, Pat, Peggy, Michelle

My Brothers
Brian, Tom, Chris

Books by Tony Marvin

The Templar Chronicles Series
Betrayal – Darkness Engulfs the Knight
Fugitives – Stripped of the Cross
Dispersion – Dawn of a New Knight

Science Fiction
The House on Crescent Street

Action-Adventure
The Making of a MERCYnary

Cover Art and Website development by:
LDerrickson Digital
www.Derricksondesign.com

Introduction

August 23, 1307

Three men sit in a small stone room; the only light comes from four candles scattered about the space. All the men appear to be in their late middle age, and although it was not the custom of the time, all three men have beards in various stages of gray. The first man, Visitor of the Templars and second-in-command of the Knights Templar, Hugh de Pairaud, has a deep scar that runs almost straight down from his scalp to the corner of his mouth on the left side of his face. He wears an eye patch over where the left eye once resided. The second man, Commander of the Vault of Acre, Admiral Gregory, who commands the vast Templar fleet, is wearing a dark brown hooded cloak. Like the cloak, this man is weatherworn but still has many years of service left. The third man, Grand Master and overall commander of the Knights Templar, Jacques de Molay, is wearing a leather gambeson that shows rust stains from the chain mail armor worn over it when needed. This man appears near exhaustion, with deep worry lines etched on his face.

In an exasperated tone, Admiral Gregory says, "Sir, we must make a decision now. King Philip is going to move against us soon. We cannot continue to wait. Every moment we waste could cost us dearly in men, money, and other items of value."

Hugh de Pairaud adds, "Grand Master, I can see only two choices. One, we move the bulk of our men and movable possessions out of France and away from King Philip's reach. Two, we establish a defensive position here in France and consolidate our forces there. Then we send delegations to the Pope and the kings in all the countries where we have commanderies outside of France and convince them to pressure the King of France to stop his activities against us."

Jacques de Molay says, "How do you propose we move all the knights, sergeants, men-at-arms, clergy, not to mention squires, blacksmiths, farmers, stable hands, scribes, and other auxiliary personnel out of France without the King's men knowing? There are sure to be spies within our organization. Guillaume de Nogaret is no fool, and I'm sure he has men who are always watching us. Besides, that would require us to abandon all our holdings here in France. We

2

cannot afford to do that; we need those lands and buildings to raise money for a new crusade."

Hugh de Pairaud says as if he hadn't heard what the Grand Master replied, "We use the fleet to move some of the men from the ports in La Rochelle and Aragon to Scotland. We have some travel over land to…"

The Grand Master interrupts in a quiet voice, "We will not run, nor will we hold up behind walls. I will speak to the Pope and King Philip myself. We do not answer to the King of France. We are subject only to God and the Holy Father himself. King Philip has no authority over us, and surely he will not move without the Pope's sanction."

After a moment of silence, he adds with little conviction in his weak voice, "Besides, I am a trusted advisor to King Philip. I believe the source of your fears is unfounded."

The other two men start arguing with Grand Master Jacques de Molay, but he silences them by slamming his large and still-powerful fist onto the writing table at his side. His voice now rises in force, making it clear to the other two who is in charge, "I have moved the bulk of our treasury to safer locations in case King Philip is foolish enough to move against us. I will also have the items that have caused great concern among the two of you transported to a secret location that has already been prepared. Rest easy, gentlemen; I would die before I see this Order discredited. I will take care of this. I appreciate your concern, but I believe King Philip is not so ignorant as to act in such a rash manner. He may not be overly fond of us Templars at the present time, but he must see he has no reason or authority to move against us."

With that, the two men knew the discussion was over, and they were excused. They silently exit the Grand Master's chambers. As they walk the hallways of the Paris commandery, Hugh de Pairaud says, "I think the Grand Master's belief that King Philip will wait for the Pope is incorrect. This Pope is little more than a captive of the King. King Philip believes he can remove us from his lands and confiscate everything the Order owns.

"Additionally, the Crown of France owes us a great deal of money that was borrowed to support France's war with England. I fear his belief that all will be well is misplaced. I will move as many men as I can legitimately transfer out of France."

Admiral Gregory replies, "My ships are at your disposal, but you must act soon. I have already issued orders that will keep only a few ships in the French ports. I have made contact with a few men I know in various locations to aid us if the need arises. I wish I knew where the Grand Master was transferring the item of primary concern in case anything was to happen to him. If he won't tell us, who will he tell?"

Chapter 1

William de Sevrey was twenty years old with auburn-colored hair and a beard that was having great difficulty getting beyond the patchy stage. He was slightly taller than average, although thin, his muscles were well-corded from years of training. William hurried as rapidly as he could through the dimly lit halls on his way to his second meeting with Grand Master Jacques de Molay. He recalled his first meeting, as it was just over two months ago. As a young Knight of the Temple, it was a great honor to have a private meeting with the Grand Master. Of course, William was the great-nephew of Peter de Sevrey and, therefore, had a certain standing regardless of being knighted just two years ago.

Peter de Sevrey had been the Marshal of the Templars in 1291, who, at the fall of Acre, is rumored to have secretly removed a sacred treasure from under the nose of the Sultan Khalil. There were only a few Templars left to defend the last section of the once-strong castle. These Templars were the last holdouts of what had been a cooperative force of several crusading armies; all the other crusading armies had escaped by ship as the Sultan's army began to overpower the defenses. The remaining Templars, led by Peter de Sevrey gave their heads to buy more time for the Treasurer of the Templars to make good his escape with the object.

At Williams' first meeting with Jacques de Molay, the Grand Master was friendly. William noticed he asked many questions regarding his belief in God, trust in the Templar organization, and faith in his Holy calling as a Poor Knight of the Temple of Solomon. The meeting ended abruptly when William said he would gladly give his life to preserve the Order as his great-uncle had done. As soon as he made the comment, William realized his statement was full of pride and arrogance, and it displayed his youth and stupidity like a banner flapping in the wind.

When William arrived at the Grand Master's door this time, he hesitated before knocking. His initial thought was to smack the wooden door three times, hard with his fist, to demonstrate his self-confidence. Then, he thought that possibly, such an act might be construed as disrespectful. Ultimately, he knocked firmly but no harder than needed to be heard. In a clear but tired voice, the Grand Master told William to enter.

5

Jacques de Molay's room was no different from any other knight's quarters, except that he had the room to himself; all the other knights shared their rooms with a fellow knight. It was furnished with a straw-filled bed, chair, small writing table (although most of the knights, including the Grand Master, were nearly illiterate), and a wooden chest in which the knight kept the few items the Order entrusted to their keeping. In addition to these furnishings, a large wooden crate was present in the room. This crate had not been in the Grand Master's chamber during William's previous visit and apparently was not generally in the quarters, for it took up a large portion of the floor space. There was so little open floor space that William and the Grand Master were forced to conduct their meeting crowded near the table.

Jacques greeted William cordially, but there was an anxious tension in the air that William could almost see. After brief pleasantries, Jacques got right to the point. "Sir William, I have a mission for you. It is the most important endeavor you will likely be involved in. It is also crucial to the Order that you succeed in this task. I need you to travel to the small village of Rennes-le-Chateau in Southern France. There, you will meet a priest whom you are to give this letter and the contents of this crate." Jacques indicated a parchment sealed with the Grand Master's mark and the large chest in the middle of the room.

"May I ask what is in the box, sir?" William asked.

To William's astonishment, Jacques snapped in quick anger, "You may not! You are to carry out your orders! You are not to look in the box, and the letter must arrive with the seal unbroken. You are to protect both items with your life." Then Jacques visibly softened and, with a look of shame, said, "I'm sorry. I haven't slept well lately. Sir William, I chose you specifically for this job for several reasons. I'm afraid I can't reveal many details of why you need to follow these orders, but know this: the future of the Templars may depend on what you do."

"Yes, sir, I will not let you or the Order down," William responded in a chastened tone.

The Grand Master regained his commanding voice and said, "Of course. Now, as to the company you are to take. I want you to take Sir Henry de Craon, Sergeant Bertrand, three war horses, six riding horses, four mules, a wagon, Thomas the priest, and two squires of your choosing." William was not entirely pleased to hear who his companions would be. Sir Henry was not a friend of William's, but they got along well enough.

On the other hand, Sergeant Bertrand was one of the old soldiers who had fought in the Holy Lands. He seemed more interested in drinking with a couple of the other Templars who had been to Outremer than anything else. The Sergeant made William and the other young knights feel as if they were beneath his notice.

William was trying to decide how best to broach this when Jacques de Molay said, "I know Sergeant Bertrand is not highly thought of by many here, but he is a skilled warrior and one of only a handful in Paris who is battle-tested. I know he tends to drink a bit, but he is the person I trust the most when things get difficult. Now, I will have the contents in this box loaded into a large crate and sealed shut, waiting on a wagon after Matins prayers tomorrow morning. You are excused from all duties and services for the rest of the day to prepare. I will meet you at the wagon before sunup and give you the letter then."

Knowing he had just been excused, William said, "I will not let you down, sir," and then recalled he had already said that.

"I know you won't, my son, but it's not me you need to worry about disappointing. I'll see you in the morning."

Chapter 2

William walked to the practice yard to find Sir Henry. He knew he would be there. Henry practiced every spare minute he had; if he could, he would skip prayers to swing a practice sword. Sir Henry was a couple of years older than William and stood an inch or two shorter. Henry had long, dark hair and a perfect beard. Henry was more thickly muscled than William. Even with the added bulk, Henry was still quicker and more agile with the sword than William.

Sir Henry was the fifth son of the Duke of Craon. Being the fifth son meant there was no land left for his father to give him, and he would have to find his own. Joining the Knights Templar had been his father's idea. He hoped his son would eventually travel to the Holy Land and attain enough glory to make a name for himself and perhaps gain land in the Kingdom of Jerusalem. However, that seemed unlikely now with the loss of Acre and Ruad.

The Templars no longer even had a foothold in the Holy Lands. There was always talk of a new Crusade, but popular support was lacking, which infuriated Henry. He was one of the best swordsmen in the Order and could sit a horse with the best knights in France. His bravery and skill had never been called into question. Still, his lack of wisdom and compassion always kept him in hot water with Grand Master Jacques de Molay. Henry was also a vocal supporter of combining the Hospitaller and Templar Orders. He felt this would increase the chance for a new crusade, which he saw as his only hope of gaining lands of his own. The Grand Master was steadfastly against combining the two Orders. Many felt that this was because it was more likely the Hospitallers would end up with overall command of the combined Orders, which Jacques de Molay could not abide.

William watched as Henry attacked the pell (a twelve-inch-thick log buried so that six feet of the log stuck out of the ground) as if his lead-filled wooden practice sword could destroy the thick post. When Henry finally grew so fatigued that he knew his attack lacked control and ferocity, he stopped, walked to a bucket of cold water, and plunged his head in. As he flung his head back, water flew in an arc from his hair and beard.

William approached him and said, "Sir Henry, Grand Master Jacques de Molay has given us a mission." Saying the mission has been given to "us" was a move calculated to soothe the wrath of Henry. Henry felt that he should be in charge of the endeavors they undertook as a group due to his proven skill with sword and lance. And it would have angered him if he knew he was to go along in support of William, not as equal in command.

"What scullery maid's task is that old fart sending us on this time?" Henry retorted.

Not taking the bait, William said, "We are to transport an item of importance of the Order to the village of Rennes-le-Chateau."

"And how many knights and men-at-arms are going to travel with us to protect this important item?" Henry said sardonically.

"He felt you and I would be sufficient as knights; Sergeant Bertrand will also accompany us. We are also to bring one squire each. Also, there is a priest, Thomas, who will be joining us."

"It must be very important if it is protected by only two knights and a drunken sergeant-at-arms."

Again, not taking the bait, William continued, "We are to leave after early morning prayers tomorrow. You are excused from all prayers, services, and other duties to allow time for preparation. Do you know anything about this priest or where I can find him?"

Henry, not really paying attention, said, "What? Oh, Father Thomas, yes, I know a little about him. He is old, scrawny, and will slow us down. I would look for him in the chapel library. Now, I will continue practicing since I am excused from prayers. It will help the brothers learn tolerance to hear me striking this log while they pray."

William made his way to the chapel library to find the priest. At first, William thought the library was empty. Then he noticed a man sitting at a desk in a far corner studying what appeared to be an ancient scroll. The man matched Sir Henry's description of Thomas, and William knew he had found his priest. Thomas was indeed scrawny. William had seen men with more meat on them who had just recovered from dysentery.

William approached as quietly as he could, but his leather boots creaked, and his sword clanked in its scabbard as he approached the hunched-over figure. Having gotten within a few

9

feet of the priest, William cleared his throat. He felt very self-conscious in this quiet place. Thomas raised his right hand slowly and extended his long, bony index finger, indicating that William should wait until he finished what he was reading.

After many minutes, Thomas lowered his hand. Without turning to face William, he said, "I know why you are here, Sir William de Sevrey. Grand Master Jacques had informed me of our mission some time ago, to give me adequate time to learn what I needed to know. I will meet you in the morning." Then Thomas returned to his reading.

Sir William waited an awkward moment, then slowly turned and walked out without saying a word, feeling even more confused than when he had been excused from the Grand Master's quarters.

Next, William needed to seek out Sergeant Bertrand. He knew where Bertrand would be. The few veterans of Outremer were always in the same location when not carrying out duties for the Grand Master or overseeing the training of knights, squires, and sergeants-at-arms on how to fight as a unit. Most armies fought as a mass of individual warriors, especially knights. A heavy cavalry charge may start as a line of knights, sergeant-at-arms, and squires on horseback. However, as soon as the horses began to move at a canter, the line dissolved into an unruly wave. Once the horses reached a gallop, it was just a mass of individuals. Even with this mob formation, the weight of horse and rider smashing into the enemy devastated those on the receiving end. But the Templars had learned that if they attacked as a unit, they could multiply the impact of their attack. To achieve this, the soldiers needed to learn to move as one and maintain uniformity in their weapons and armor, allowing them to remain flexible in the event of losses.

Each soldier, whether a knight, sergeant, or squire, would be armored in a mail hauberk covering his torso, arms, and upper legs. A chainmail coif would protect the head and neck, leaving the face exposed. Then, a helmet would be placed over the top of the coif, covering the entire head except for small eye slits. A large heater shield would also be carried. The knights would have worn a white surcoat with a red Templar cross. The sergeants would have worn a black surcoat with a red cross. The knights, sergeants, and squires would all have had a lance, a sword, and a dagger; occasionally, war hammers were also used.

Fighting in the Holy Lands, they quickly learned that you couldn't keep a hundred galloping horses in formation. With that many individual moving pieces, any organized change in direction was nearly impossible. The Templar's solution was to train and fight in manageable-sized groups of three to five knights or sergeants-at-arms, each having one or two squires, and each member armed and armored the same. These groups would maintain a "V" formation as they reached a gallop and smashed into the enemy line. This group of between six and fifteen heavily armed and armored soldiers would sweep through the enemy and continue straight for fifty to one hundred feet. Slowing to a canter, they would wheel right and reform the "V," stopping to fill in gaps for those who may have fallen, and then charge the line again. The next time they wheeled, it would be to the left after puncturing the line. By doing this, they would work their way down the line. This type of attack forced the enemy to constantly turn 180 degrees and then reset to receive the next charge, resulting in widespread confusion among their foes. Sergeant Bertrand told them that when it was done properly, it was like stitching with a needle and thread, and he would call them his "little seamstresses in training." Depending upon the size of the battle, there could be many of these "V" formations cutting enormous swaths out of the enemy with every pass.

Sergeant Bertrand was often in charge of the training sessions and had little patience for anyone who could not handle his horse with absolute control. He constantly told them that the controlled formation of horses and riders did more damage than any flailing about of swords or lances. He often berated them by saying that if he could train the horses to charge the line without the damn fool riders, he could save the Templars a fortune in training and maintaining knights.

Sergeant Bertrand was old, at least fifty. He was of average height, five feet five inches, with broad shoulders and almost no neck. He was deeply tanned so that his skin appeared like leather. His cold glare could make the biggest of men stop in their tracks. William had only seen him bested once in the training yard, and that was by Henry. Bertrand took the loss with unexpected courtesy and congratulated Henry for his skill at arms. The next day, Henry faced Sergeant Bertrand again. This time, Henry found himself on his back with the Sergeant's practice sword at his neck within the first few moments of the contest. Bertrand was short-tempered and condescending to any of the young knights and many of the older knights who had never left the French commanderies to fight in Outremer. He was thick-muscled and had a voice that sounded like he chewed thistles. All the young knights complained about the lack of respect he showed them, but no one ever complained to him personally. Only once did a knight dare to complain to the Grand Master. That knight was made responsible for ensuring the stables were clean for the following six months.

William found Bertrand chatting with one of the cooks behind the kitchen, a man who had also been in Outremer as one of the hundreds of support staff. This cook was the only man, besides Grand Master Jacques, that William had ever seen Bertrand speak to "socially." As William approached, both men stopped talking and looked at him as if he were disturbing them.

William self-consciously cleared his throat and said, "Sergeant Bertrand, Grand Master Jacques has given me a mission that you are to be a part of." Bertrand continued to stare at him. "Umm, we are to transport an object to the village of Rennes-le-Chateau. We will be leaving in the morning following early morning prayers." Bertrand stared at William as if waiting for him to say something more. William finally said, "Well, okay, I will see you in the morning." William felt their eyes following him as he turned and left, but neither man made a sound while William was still in earshot. He was glad that was over with. Now, he needed to get his squire, Louis, and see to his horses and equipment.

Chapter 3

William had to go searching for Louis. He should have been in the stables caring for the horses, but he was not there. William went to the armory, thinking maybe Louis was there, but again he was not. He asked some of the other squires, but none that he came across had seen Louis since breakfast. Then, William ran into one of the younger squires, whom Louis often talked into mischief. The boy was in a hurry and a bit nervous, a clear sign Louis had him running an errand. William placed both hands on the young lad's shoulders and said, "Boy, where are you off to in such a hurry? If you feed me a pack of lies, I'll make sure you spend every moment you are not in prayer working the bellows for the blacksmith."

The boy stammered, "I'm just on my way to the stables for… some manure… to help… um … fertilize Father Falaradeau's… um… roses."

"I see," said William, knowing that although the boy was telling the truth, he was still lying. "Did Father Falaradeau send you on this task, or is manure gathering your idea?"

The boy looked down at his shoes and almost whispered, "Um… it was Louis' idea."

"That is as I had supposed. I assume Louis is waiting at the rose garden for you?" To which the boy nodded. William continued, "I'm sure Father Falaradeau would like to know all about these improvements you boys have planned for his private garden. I want you to go to him now and tell him what you were planning on doing and ask his penance."

At this, the boy looked terrified but said, "Father Falaradeau is gone on church business until the day after tomorrow."

William recalled that the good Father was gone and said, "Then you are to go to your chamber now and pray to the Virgin for forgiveness and administer your own penance. If I see you anywhere not praying or working for your master during the next two weeks, I will know you have underestimated your sin. Now go!"

William, fighting to suppress a grin, headed for Father Falaradeau's garden. The Father oversaw the spiritual education of the squires. He had to be at least seventy and was very free with using the lash to drive a point home with the boys. His garden was the only thing the man seemed to have tender feelings for. It was a walled-in flower garden that he lovingly cared for. William knew Father Falaradeau had become increasingly mean-spirited toward those under his spiritual guidance as he grew older and his vision diminished. Since he could not see well, he assumed that the boys under his charge were continually making fun of him, a belief that was likely very accurate. The good Father enjoyed giving the boys unachievable tasks and then doling out harsh punishment when they weren't completed on time. The knights, tired of their squires having to write out Latin prayers when they should be cleaning rust off mail or practicing with the sword, had finally convinced the Grand Master that the Father should be relieved of his educational duties. Father Falaradeau would be informed of this change in responsibilities upon his return from his trip.

William strode to the garden gate and heard several boys talking and laughing inside the walls. Chief among the voices was Louis. Louis was an older squire, seventeen years old, and was of a height with William. Louis was thinner, and although he appeared lightly muscled, he performed surprisingly well with the sword and on horseback. Louis always seemed to be sunburned and had hair bleached blond by the sun. He was friendly with everyone and equally mischievous. Louis was standing in a wheelbarrow, giving orders as if the other squires scurrying around the garden were his army. "Move that red one over there. No, no, more to the right, that's it."

William silently opened the gate. For a moment, no one noticed him. They were all intent on their work. There must have been fifteen boys crowded in the small garden. They were transplanting flowers of many colors to various locations within the low stone wall. For a moment, William thought they might be doing a good deed. The flowers were being handled with utmost care. The boys were planting the flowers, carefully smoothing out the dirt, and rearranging the stones for the gravel path that wound among them. Then, William saw the bigger picture. In the center of the most massive rose patch, the boys were transplanting the yellow roses to spell out in Latin "DEVILS' EXCREMENT." They were carefully planting the red roses around the yellow ones so that once completed, you could only tell what was "written" there if you stood on the garden wall and looked down.

14

William finally said, in a loud voice, "Louis, have you not yet learned that when you do a job that requires secrecy, the first thing you should do is post a guard and have a way of escape established?" At the sound of his voice, the boys all froze. The laughing suddenly stopped; truth be told, some of them manufactured their own fertilizer right then. William continued with as much ice in his voice as he could muster, "Louis, you will come with me now. The rest of you will return all the flowers to their original location. Then, you will ensure that all evidence of your presence is removed. If Father Falaradeau notices anything out of the ordinary in this garden, I will make sure he is fully aware of each of your names." With that, he turned and walked out of the garden.

Louis was the third son of a minor noble house in the Champagne region of France. He was very close to attaining his spurs and becoming a knight himself. It had been discussed several times to send Louis to the King's castle to be knighted. He met every requirement necessary to become a member of the chivalry, but there always seemed to be a disciplinary issue that held him up.

The Templars could not make him a knight themselves, but they could recommend him. If a man wanted to become a Knight Templar, he had to be knighted before joining the Order. Then, following his knighthood, he had to accept the additional responsibilities and restrictions of being a monk. The Templars did take young men of noble birth as squires. If a squire performed well, he would be recommended to a monarch or other political leader with authority to bestow a knighthood. Then, the newly created knight could choose whether he wished to join the Templars and take the Holy Orders of a monk.

Louis appeared to be in a state of panic and shock. He started toward the gate to follow William, stopped upon reaching the gate, turned back toward the garden, and said, "Do as he says, lads, or there will be Hell... or worse yet, Heaven to pay!"

Louis quickly caught up with William and said, "It was just a bit of harmless fun. With his vision being as bad as it is, he would never have noticed. We had to do something! Father Falaradeau gave us a sermon by Saint Bernard to memorize word for word in the week he was to be gone. We have to learn it in Latin. He said any of us who do not have it seared in our hearts by the time he returns would be put on latrine duty permanently."

William said, "You may wish you were only assigned to latrine duty by the time I'm done with you. You not only organized an assault on a man of God, but you failed to do your work as my squire. I am to leave on an important mission for the Order, and there is much to be done. I am to take a squire with me and had planned on bringing you, but now I believe I will have to look to another."

Louis nearly stumbled over a rock on the ground. True regret finally showed in his expression and could be heard in his voice: "I'm very sorry, Sir William. It won't happen again; the devil got the better of my anger. I understand if you must leave me behind. I know I'm not as good as I should be, but I'm not as bad as I could be either, and that should account for something."

Still outwardly displaying the anger he did not feel, William said, "We will see how well and quickly you prepare my horses and armor and gather the supplies we will need. Louis, I am disappointed in you. You really should not have been caught."

Chapter 4

William got little sleep that night. He worried about every detail of preparing for the trip. It should take only a few weeks to reach Rennes-le-Chateau. The roads were good most of the way there, unless it rained. He'd need to be sure they had extra oiled canvases to protect the crate and their armor, another job for when he got up. He also wondered why they were going to a town as remote as Rennes-le-Chateau. He knew the Order had some type of establishment there since laborers, carpenters, and masons from the Paris commandery were sometimes sent there to work. Almost a year ago, he had asked a master carpenter he was acquainted with what they were doing there. The carpenter said that he was not allowed to say, but that William would not believe him even if he did tell him. And that cryptic response was all he ever got.

William finally gave up trying to sleep around two in the morning. He decided to get up and attend to all the little details that had been bothering him while he tried to sleep. He spent most of the time reviewing their supplies and adding the items he thought of while lying awake in bed. William was grateful to see Louis also awake, outside rolling his chainmail in a barrel of sand to remove the rust. Louis had already brushed down and checked the horses and mules for the trip. William decided to attend Matins even though he didn't have to. For the first time in many years, William sincerely desired to pray, but his prayers seemed to go nowhere. All he felt was increasing anxiety about his upcoming mission.

William met with the rest of his party down by the stables. Everything was ready by the time he arrived. Louis and Odo, Henry's Squire, had the horses prepared and the knight's gear packed. Jacques de Molay was talking in hushed tones with Sergeant Bertrand. The priest, Thomas, was already seated on the back of a horse and seemed lost in prayer or thought. Sir Henry was sitting on an empty cask that lay on its side against a wall, repeatedly throwing his long knife in the dirt at his feet, acting thoroughly bored. The wagon, hitched to two mules, was loaded with a much larger crate than what was in the Grand Master's room. The crate was covered with an oiled canvas and chained closed. The extra horses for William, Henry, and Bertrand were tied to the back of the wagon.

Finally, Grand Master Jacques de Molay stopped talking with Bertrand and said in a commanding voice, "I am sending you men on a critical mission. This crate is to be protected at all times and must not be opened under any circumstances. Although you ride well-traveled roads in friendly territory, stay alert as bandits may be tempted to attack even Templars. Your goal is to make sure your charge arrives safely." Then he walked up to William and said so that only William could hear him, "Here is the key to the lock for the chains on the crate and a letter for the priest in Rennes-le-Chateau. His name is Father Lull. He is of the Cistercian Order and not a member of the Templars, but he has my full confidence. If he needs your assistance, you are to give it without hesitation. By the time you reach him, it is possible, although unlikely, that certain complications may have arisen. If this happens, you must trust Father Thomas and Father Lull just as you would trust me. No matter what happens, do not lose faith in our Order, the Church, or our Holy Father, the Pope."

William was a little concerned by this final comment, but did not know what to say or even precisely why it bothered him. After a pause, William finally replied, "Of course, sir. You can count on me. I mean us. We will not let you, the Order, nor the Holy Father down." William felt like an imbecile for repeatedly telling the Grand Master that he 'would not let him down.' Jacques de Molay nodded and, with a tired, almost fearful look, turned and walked away.

As William watched him walk slowly, he had the odd feeling that he should say something that would encourage the leader of the Templars. But he did not know what to say or even what it was that hung like a dark veil over Jacques de Molay. The man appeared to have aged years in recent months. The weight of some unwanted responsibility hung from his shoulders, slowing his every step.

The small band of Templars was quiet as they made their way through Paris. There were few people out in the streets at this pre-dawn hour. Those few they did encounter moved obligingly aside to let members of the Templars pass. Once they were out of the city and in the country, everyone's mood began to brighten. The sun was rising, and it appeared the day would be excellent for travel.

Louis was the first to break the silence. "What a beautiful day! And just think, Odo, no prayers today."

With a sharp look, Thomas said, "Young man, you should always be praying. It is an honor that God would take the time to listen to you."

With only the hint of a grin, Louis said, "You are quite right, Father. Thank you for that chastisement. My times in prayer are the sweetest moments of my miserable life. I am glad that the Grand Master was wise enough to send a spiritual guide like yourself along so that the rest of this carnal company do not lead impressionable young men like Odo and me astray." Thomas, who thought he was being made fun of but was not confident enough to confront Louis, merely grunted and turned to look back down the road.

"So, Odo, what do you think the Grand Master has entrusted us to pack all the way to southern France?" Louis asked.

Embarrassed to be the center of attention for even the briefest moments, Odo said, "I haven't thought about it."

Excitedly, Louis said, "You're kidding? That is all I've thought about since I saw the big crate under the tarpaulin. Do you think it could be full of gold? It could be the Crown Jewels of France or England; I'd heard we Templars protect them. Or perhaps it's a sacred relic brought back from the Holy Land. It could be the sword of St. Peter, the Ark of the Covenant, or even a piece of the True Cross."

At this last remark, Sergeant Bertrand snorted and said, "What do you know of Holy relics out of the Holy Land? Talk of the Ark of the Covenant was common in that sandy hell. Yet, real information about it was almost as elusive as piety. And as for the True Cross, if you took all the wood brought out of Outremer that was supposedly part of the True Cross, you could build a grand cathedral."

Thomas, the priest, said, "Your tone seems a bit impertinent, Sergeant. One might think you have lost faith in your Holy calling as a soldier of the Cross."

Sergeant Bertrand looked at the priest with open hatred and said, "Father, I am not foolish enough to discuss with you my faith nor my calling. I assume the Grand Master had a reason for sending you on this little trip, but I doubt it was to discuss issues of faith with me. I would prefer you refrain from speaking to me unless necessary."

The Sergeant's comment left the group uncomfortably quiet

until Louis quipped, "It's probably just a bust of Jacques de Molay anyway."

As the day wore on, clouds began to gather in the sky. A couple of hours before sunset, it was as dark as midnight. William finally called a halt, and they set up camp for the night. No sooner had Odo gotten the kindling for a fire burning than the skies opened in a downpour. They spent a cold, wet night sleeping as best they could under the wagon.

Chapter 5

The rain continued to fall the next two days, soaking the party and depressing their spirits. By late morning on the third day, Louis asked William, "Don't you think it might be a good idea to eat a warm lunch that might add a bit of heat to our bodies?"

Before William could respond, Henry said, "That is the best idea I've heard since we started this trip. I believe there's some venison that we could warm up. And a cup of warmed wine would feel rather good right now."

William looked to Sergeant Bertrand to determine what he thought, but Bertrand seemed to be paying no attention. Thomas was shivering beneath his riding cloak so much that William imagined he could hear the man's bones rattle. William said in a determined voice, as if he was making a critical decision, "That does sound good. How much dry wood do you still have in the wagon, Louis? We should reach Vezelay in a couple of days and hopefully find dry wood there if this rain continues. We need to keep enough dry wood in reserve for a fire each night until we get there."

"We have plenty," Louis responded. "We could pull up over on the right here. I'm sure there's a place where we can build a fire and lie under the wagon to get out of the rain for a minute."

They were beside the road within a few minutes, and Odo and Louis were working on starting the fire. All dismounted except for Sergeant Bertrand; he was still sitting on his horse in the middle of the road, paying little attention to the rest of the party.

Henry asked, "Do you really need to sit guard duty?"

Bertrand responded without moving or even looking in their direction, "I'm not on guard duty. I'm just not foolish enough to try to get warm. Trying to get comfortable for even a few minutes is a mistake. In weather like this, stopping only makes it harder to get started again. It makes it seem as though the discomfort has worsened. I'll sit here, eat some dried rabbit, and wait for you to try and work up the initiative to climb back in your saddles."

Henry turned back to the fire as it started to take hold, shaking his head and dismissing everything the sergeant had said as the ramblings of an old man who thinks he knows everything.

Odo was the first to hear the distant cries. It appeared to come from off in the woods on their left. The screams sounded like a woman in distress. Without waiting for the rest of the men in the party, Bertrand drew his sword and spurred his horse into the trees. He moved the horse at a walk due to the unfamiliar footing and to allow the rain to cover the sounds of his approach. As he wound his way along a deer path, he noted a small clearing where he could see ghostlike human shapes through the rain and trees. The three men were so intent on trying to hold the girl down that Sergeant Bertrand was only a few feet from them before they knew of his presence.

"I don't think the lady is of a mind to lie in the mud," Bertrand said in a voice that was little more than a growl.

All three men let go of the girl, who quickly disappeared into the surrounding brush. Each man had their weapons close at hand, and they quickly retrieved them while Bertrand watched them in an unconcerned manner. One man had a bow, another an axe, and the third a pair of short swords or long knives; Bertrand really couldn't tell which. The way they stood and spread out showed Bertrand these were not just ruffians but men whose trade was murder and robbery.

"Gentlemen, don't be fools. You have lost a few moments of fun; don't add your lives to the bill." He held the sword hilt in his right hand and let the blade rest across his saddle. Other than that, Bertrand showed no sign of being concerned by the men spreading out before him.

The man with the swords said, "There are three of us and only one of you. I dare say that your sword, armor, and horse would bring the three of us enough to live easily for a year. If only two or even one of us survives, then that means fewer to divide the spoils with."

With practiced speed, the archer nocked an arrow to the bowstring, drew, aimed at Bertrand's chest, and loosed. The man with the axe charged straight at Bertrand while the man with the swords moved further to Bertrand's right to attack from the side.

Although these tactics would likely have proved successful with a merchant or even a local Lord, they were misdirected when dealing with a man of Bertrand's experience. The arrow should have been fired at the horse, but you don't get much money for a dead horse. Bertrand's chainmail could stop an arrow with the usual field point from most bows, even at this close range. This archer's bow and string were wet, which significantly decreased the bow's power.

The man with the axe had clearly never attacked a man on a war horse. Although the average horse would panic, rear up, and possibly unhorse the rider, a destrier was trained to charge and trample men with its sharp and deadly hooves.

Bertrand's response to the attack was controlled more by muscle memory than conscious thought. As the arrow chinked harmlessly off his armor, he gave the horse its reins, allowing it to collide headlong into the man with the axe. The axe man also made the fatal error of attempting to attack the rider rather than the horse and had the life crushed out of him by 2000 pounds of horseflesh. As the horse leaped forward, Bertrand's sword rose and came crashing down on the head of the archer to his left before the man could fire a second arrow. He jerked his sword free before the gore of the man's head could grasp the blade. Bertrand quickly checked the horse's advance and spun him to the right to face the man with the swords.

The man, so confident that he would eat for the next year by just killing one man, now seemed to be in shock as his two partners in crime died so rapidly. To the highwayman's horror, two more armored men on horseback appeared. Like a rabbit who has realized it has waited for danger to get too close, he bolted headlong into the forest.

Without a word, Bertrand swung down from his horse and wiped the blood from his sword on the archer's shirt. He then inspected his horse for any harm it might have received from trampling the axe man. Finding no injury to his horse, he began to rifle the bodies of the two dead thieves.

Henry said, "What are you doing? Those men are dead. You're no better than a common highwayman yourself."

Without looking up, Bertrand said, "This is part of what happens when soldiers fight. The lofty goals to rescue the Holy Land or kill the infidel are matters for the Lords and Kings. Soldiers like me, who are not gentlemen, search the bodies of the slain, friend and foe, to get something of value that might buy us a drink or whatever other comfort we can purchase. The dead don't need their valuables. Gentlemen like yourself won't settle for small pickings such as these; your booty comes in the form of land, estates, castles, or entire countries. I won't call you a thief for stealing a kingdom from another man, and you don't call me one for liberating

23

a few coins or a trinket from a man who has no further need of it. Don't worry; if I find anything of true value, I'll turn it over to the Order as my vow of poverty requires. But if I find enough coins to cover a drink, I'll keep that for myself, so I won't have to use any of the Templar money the Grand Master gave Sir William for that evil brew."

Henry replied, "We have all taken a vow of poverty and therefore own nothing: land, castles, countries, or even a few coins."

After inspecting the archer's bow and tossing it back to the ground, Bertrand said, "Don't lecture me, boy, about things you know nothing about." Henry was clearly angry at being reproved by a sergeant that he felt was beneath him, turned and rode back to the road in silent anger.

Finding nothing valuable, Bertrand mounted his horse. As if to the woods themselves, he said, "Young lady, you had better come with us. We'll see you safely to Vezelay. One of your suitors is still among the living." He then trotted his horse back to the road.

William was still looking at the trampled remains of a man in the mud as the girl slowly came out of hiding. He did not notice her until she tentatively touched his leg. William flinched at the touch. On seeing the bruised and bleeding young lady, he quickly dismounted and helped her onto his horse. She tried to protest, but William would have none of it. "What is your name, my lady?" William asked as he helped her into the saddle.

"Mary," was the soft reply.

"You'll be safe with us, Mary. We are heading to Vezelay and should arrive in a couple of days. Or if you have a home nearby, we can see you safely there. Where are you from?"

"Nowhere. I have no home." Mary said. Not knowing what to say, William silently led the horse back to the trail where his companions waited.

Thomas was startled and then angered at the sight of the girl on Williams' horse. His face turned red as he stormed up to the girl and said, "Get off that horse, you whore! Be gone! We have no time for your snares."

William was about to strike the priest when Bertrand said, "That's right, Father, show the girl who was clearly beaten and nearly raped all the love the Church is famous for."

To this, Thomas spun around to face the sergeant and, in a

voice dripping with acid, said, "You will soon see what power the Church commands. You Templars are not beyond the power of the King. You may think you can plan your evil in your secret dark meetings, but the flames of the church will expose your wicked deeds."

This outburst surprised everyone, including Sergeant Bertrand. They all stood in silence as the priest strode over to sit beneath the wagon, leaving his back to all of them. They probably would have questioned the priest about his strange statement and accusation if it wasn't for the girl in their midst. Seeing the girl swaying in the saddle as if about to faint, Odo moved to help her down, breaking the mesmeric moment. Odo and William helped her to the fire. Henry drew a nearly dry riding cloak from his saddle pack and placed it around the girl's shoulders. Louis handed her a cup of warmed wine. Even Bertrand climbed down from his saddle and moved closer to the fire, although he focused more on the priest than the girl.

Louis was dumbstruck for one of the rare moments in his life. He would never be able to explain why. This young woman, who might not be homely beneath all the mud and detritus of the forest, was no raving beauty, yet he was strongly drawn to her. He recalled one of the few verses of Scripture he had bothered to memorize.

"O my dove, in the clefts of the rock,
In the secret place of the steep pathway,
Let me see your form,
Let me hear your voice:
For your voice is sweet,
And your form is lovely."

He had memorized that section of scripture in the hopes of using it to get some girl to have sex with him… at some future point in time. He had thought it was just a polite way of saying, "I'd like to see you naked." But now, looking at this young lady, he understood, seeing her form was not her body but her soul. Maybe it was the vulnerability of her situation, but that also did not ring entirely true. Louis had no rationale for his feelings. He just knew that he wanted to get to know this young lady.

William broke Louis' trance by telling him to get more wood

25

on the fire. He barely noticed what he was doing as he laid two more logs on the small cool fire and then began poking it with a stick until it grew in size and warmth. Louis offered her something to eat, but she declined and merely sipped at her wine. Henry asked where she was from, how she came to be on this road, and who those men were.

She replied quietly but steadily, "I was born in Orleans. My father was a carpenter, and my mother earned extra money by mending clothes for many people in the town. Both my parents died a few years ago from a fever. An aunt and uncle took me in, more to get the few possessions my parents had than out of kindness. They treated me well for a time, as well as could be expected. But recently, my uncle has been paying too much attention to me, so my aunt said it was time for me to move out. I decided to head to Paris, hoping I could find work there. I spent several weeks looking for some honorable work but could find none. I had run out of the little money I had, and with nowhere else to turn, I went to a church to pray. I met a priest who listened to my story with kindness. He said he knew a Lord who had mentioned he was looking for servants for his winter home. He told me to return the next day. I returned each day for the next three days, but each time, the priest said the gentleman had not reappeared yet and that I should return the following day. On the fourth day, I was about to give up and leave Paris, but the priest told me he had finally spoken to the Lord, and he had agreed to meet with me the next morning. I cleaned myself up as best I could and returned to the church at sunrise. The priest introduced me to Lord du Morvan, who said his Lady needed a maid in their winter house in Beaune. He seemed like a very nice, quiet gentleman. Since I had no other choice, I took the position. He gave me a few coins to buy some food, as my stomach was growling while he spoke to me. He told me to meet him two days later at the livery beside his home in Paris.

"Since there was just one carriage, he had me ride inside with him. Before we had even left the city, he told me I smelled worse than the barn animals and that, as the day warmed, it would grow so bad that it would overpower his sensitive nature. He told the driver to stop at the next decent tavern that advertised rooms for rent. When we halted, he instructed the coachman to have the tavern keeper prepare a bath, preferably with unused, warm water. He then

26

told me to get inside and remove the rags I called clothes and to wash the filth from my body.

"I'd never taken a bath in a real tub. It was the most delightful thing I have ever experienced. Sitting in that warm water was so…comforting. I was thinking about how I never wanted to get out of the water when Lord du Morvan burst into the room. I was utterly overcome with shame and tried to cover myself, but he seemed not to notice. The Lord held a new dress out for me to see and said that I was to put it on when I was done. He then, for the first time, looked at me, trying to cover myself in the tub, and seemed to notice my nakedness. Raising his eyebrows, Lord du Morvan commented that this winter might not be so dull after all. He laid the dress across the back of a chair and left the room. As uncertain as I was about the situation, I could think of nothing else to do, so I climbed from the now-tepid water and put on the dress. The dress was nothing fancy, just plain cheap spun wool. But it was new and clean and had been dyed white, so it wasn't the same brown-gray as all the previous dresses I had ever owned. Being clean and in a new dress was…so…crisp, like I was a whole new person. But it didn't stay that way.

"We stopped in Melun, where Lord du Morvan had a friend. I was allowed to sleep with the house servants on a straw-filled cot that night. The next morning, we resumed our journey. For the next two days, it rained. I spent my time in the carriage while Lord du Morvan talked to me about his lands, his family, and how cruel the world was to those without someone powerful and strong to protect them.

"Yesterday, the rain cleared briefly, and the sun shone. Lord du Morvan had the driver stop the carriage and instructed him and the coachman to prepare lunch in a clearing nearby. As preparations for his lunch were carried out, he talked to me about how invaluable he was to the king and his considerable influence in the kingdom. I believed most of it was just men's bragging, but I smiled and acted awed by his self-possessing power. All the while, I wished the preparations for his lunch would finish so I could get away from him and eat the old bread, sour wine, and perhaps some of the salted meat he gave us servants to eat. With the ground so wet, they had to set up a small table and two chairs; the cook struggled to start a fire to prepare the meal.

"To my astonishment, when his lunch was prepared, he asked if I would join him. I could not say no, even if I wanted to. I could smell the roasted pheasant from the carriage and craved the well-prepared food. The meal was the best of my life. Besides the pheasant were apples, sweet wine, soft bread, and pastries that I cannot name. He talked the whole time through the meal, but I never heard a word. I was lost in the food, such exquisite food. I was eating one of those unnamed pastries when I noticed Lord du Morvan had gotten up from his chair and stood beside me. He held out his hand, and as I tentatively placed my hand in his waiting paw and stood, he stepped closer so that he was pressed against me. Then, before I could react, his mouth covered mine. I tried to push him away, but he held me tight. His hand went to my neck, and I thought he intended to choke me, but then he tore open the front of my dress and forced me to the wet grass, straining to get on top of me. I began to struggle more and somehow must have struck him with my head because suddenly, blood was gushing from his nose all over my once-white dress. In that instant, I slipped from beneath him, got to my feet, and ran for the woods. He tried to chase me, but he soon gave up. I hid in a thicket a little distance from the clearing and waited.

"He called to me for a while, saying all would be forgiven if I came out of hiding. Soon, his offer of forgiveness turned to threats of abandoning me to this wilderness, then to silence. Shortly after that, I heard the carriage pull away. Then it started to rain again.

"I stayed the night in the thicket, afraid to move out for fear that he would be standing there. In the morning, I finally left my cover, walked back to the road, and started walking back toward Paris. I had covered very little ground when those three men came out of the woods. At first, I thought it was Lord du Morvan, but they were worse. Before they could remove their breeches, you showed up and saved me."

William said, "It was not we that saved you, but him." At this, he indicated Sergeant Bertrand, who appeared not to be listening as he stared at the priest.

Chapter 6

Saturday, Oct. 14th, 1307

Thankfully, the rain stopped the day after Mary joined their little band. Louis constantly tried to engage Mary in conversation as she rode beside him and Odo in the wagon, but to little effect. Mary was polite and laughed at his many and varied jokes, even though she was the only one who did, yet she seemed to hold little interest in talking with Louis. Louis noticed that Mary seemed to be more interested in trying to draw Odo out of his quiet shell by attempting to get him to talk about himself. At one point, Mary asked Odo where he grew up as a child. And Louis laughed and said, "Odo was never a kid; he doesn't know how to have fun; he was born the quiet, boring young man seated next to you." Odo seemed to pay no attention to the comment, but Mary gave Louis a look of anger that surprised and shamed him. He tried to make up for it by apologizing, saying he was only kidding and that Odo was a good buddy, but Mary refused to speak to him the rest of the day.

Three days later, the group of Templars and Mary reached the town of Vezelay just before the sun set. They intended to find a place to get a meal and sleep. Perhaps they would gather a few provisions, and in the morning, they could visit the local church to see if the priest knew of any work available for Mary. Before they continued their journey south, Thomas also wanted to visit the Shrine of Mary Magdalene near Vezelay.

They came to a tavern with a livery and a sign that offered rooms. They left their horses, mules, and wagon under the watch of Odo and Louis in the stable while the rest went into the tavern. Louis called out as they walked away, "Don't forget us hungry servants in the stable when you order food."

None of them noticed in the fading light the look of shock they received from the two men they passed on their way into the tavern. Nor did they see when the men hurried off down the street after they walked by. The band entered the tavern looking forward to good food, wine, and a bed on which to sleep. William was saying how much bread he was planning on eating when they noticed everyone in the tavern was staring at them as though they were brigands about to rob the place. Henry said loudly, "We're looking for food and rooms."

But no one seemed to hear him. For a few long seconds, no one spoke. Then, a man in the corner said, "Vermin!" And spat on the floor. Others started murmuring in a menacing tone, and several crossed themselves.

In a low voice, Sergeant Bertrand said, "I think maybe we should leave this place, my friends."

All seemed to agree, except Henry, who said, "We have nothing to fear from this rabble."

Bertrand leaned close to Henry and said, "Young man, do you really want to get in a fight with unarmed common men, women, and children? Would you swing your Templar sword, which is sworn to protect the helpless against them? Rabble has a way of quickly turning into an angry mob that, even though unarmed, can do considerable damage by their sheer numbers. Now, let's go."

They backed out of the Tavern and made their way to the stable. Once they stepped through the stable doors, they found the local seneschal and five other men standing by their wagon with various weapons in hand. Louis and Odo stood in the back of the wagon with looks of bewilderment and daggers in their hands. They could also hear the voices of more townspeople converging on the spot. William held his hands out to show he held no weapon and said to the seneschal, "Sir, I'm not sure what is going on here, but we are Knights Templar. We are not looking for trouble. We will get our possessions and be on our way."

"I'm afraid not, young man." the seneschal said. "The King has given me orders to arrest all the members of your Order and send them on to Paris to be questioned. Now, I'd like you to take your swords, knives, and any other weapons you carry and lay them on the ground. You and the other knight can give me your word of honor not to run, and I won't have you bound, but the others will have to be tied up."

"You can't trust their word!" declared one of the men carrying a fire-hardened wooden spear who stood beside the seneschal. "They're in league with the Devil."

"Quiet! Nothing has been proven yet, and I doubt it will be. I've friends who are Templars, and they are no more a heretic than you or I."

William, confused by all that was transpiring, said, "Sir, I'm sure there's been a mistake. We have been sent by the head of our Order to deliver some items to a priest at another one of our establishments. We want no trouble, but I'll not lay down my sword. If you and I could discuss this privately, I'm sure…"

But at that instant, one of the townspeople leaped onto the wagon and began to struggle with Odo. Another townsman yelled, "I wonder what the heretics have hidden in the box they have chained closed."

Seeing the growing number of people surging toward the wagon, William drew his sword. He advanced toward the wagon, yelling, "Get down from there! That is the property of the Templars."

The seneschal, forced to react, advanced with his men and was bolstered by the crowd of people crammed into the stable, who were adding their weight to the fight. But the Templars, being the best-trained warriors in Europe, attacked the untrained and, for the most part, unarmed people of Vezelay. William struggled to reach the crate while trying not to injure anyone seriously. He waded through the people to the wagon without doing more than just rapping a few skulls with the pommel of his sword. But once he tried to climb on the wagon, the five or six men struggling with Odo and Louis started to fight to keep him from climbing up. These men on the wagon believed they had a fortune in gold that the Templars were reputed to have in their possession. Louis and Odo were struggling as best they could to keep more men and women from climbing on the wagon. The townspeople who had gained the wagon had no real weapons, but a pitchfork could kill a man as quickly as a sword.

On William's first attempt to climb onto the wagon, a man swung a hoe at his head. William had to release his handhold to avoid the blow and stumbled backward. He then quickly lunged forward, grabbed the man who had swung the hoe by the pant leg, and pulled his leg out from under him. William then leaped onto the wagon and used his sword's pommel to knock several villagers off their feet. Each time he removed a man, two more appeared to take his place. So focused were the men on removing him from the wagon that they had stopped trying to break the chain that protected the crate. In the din and confusion, William heard Louis cry out a warning to him. William spun around just in time to see a man swing a scythe at him. Instinct took over at that moment—an instinct based on hundreds of hours of training and basic human survival. William's sword swung in a blocking blow into the scythe. Then, using the momentum gained in the parry, he reversed the sword's direction and landed a cut deep into the man's neck; the man's eyes looked in disbelief for a moment at William, and then the light of life in his eyes faded and went out. The man fell to the ground in a limp heap. The man's body was soon out of sight as more of the frenzied crowd rushed at William. In a rage, he started shoving more townspeople off the wagon.

Two of the men-at-arms who had boarded the wagon faced William with swords drawn. William realized he could not push these men off and was forced to fight them. Instead of attacking him in any coordinated attack, one attempted a straight thrust at his midsection. William easily knocked the man's sword point to the ground. He then stepped forward onto the flat of the blade with his foot, forcing it out of the man's grip. William smashed the man in the face with his fist so hard that he fell backward off the wagon and into the crowd. William then turned to the other man. This one seemed to consider retreating for a moment, but then attacked with a wildly out-of-control overhead slash at William's head. William stepped to one side, allowing the weight of the man's attack to carry him past him. He then smacked the man on the back of his head with the flat of his sword, toppling him off the wagon.

As William turned around, he realized that the townspeople were starting to leave the livery. They had realized they were losing the fight they thought would be easy and needed to reassess the situation. As the crowd rapidly retreated from the stables, William saw that the seneschal was still there. He had his sword drawn and held it out in front of him, facing Bertrand, who had his sword pointed down toward the ground but fixed his eyes on the seneschal.

Bertrand said, "Sir, I think the fight has gone out of the townspeople; two of your men-at-arms appear to be dead, and the others are unconscious or have fled. I believe it would be wise to lower that sword and withdraw."

The seneschal said, "I know it would be wise, but I cannot. I was given a charge from the King, signed by Guillaume de Nogaret. I must arrest you or die trying. Will you surrender?"

32

"I'm afraid that is not possible. We also have our orders."

"I figured as much." At that, he raised the sword blade to his face in a salute. Bertrand responded in like, and before the seneschal could react, Bertrand stepped to the man's left with unexpected speed. In the same instant, he swung his blade in a wide arch that took his sword to the left and past the seneschal's head. Bertrand, in one fluid motion, pivoted his wrist, maintaining the momentum of the blade as it swung around behind the seneschal's head and drove the sharp edge halfway through the back of his skull. The seneschal was dead before he even realized the fight had started.

Bertrand quickly jerked the weapon free of the bone and gore. He then picked up some straw and wiped the bulk of blood from the blade. Without looking at the others, he said. "Don't return your swords to their scabbards until you've completely cleaned them, or you'll be fighting to remove your sword from a scabbard crusted with dried blood when your life depends on it. Let's get the horses and mules and move out."

No one spoke as they quickly ensured that none of them were seriously injured and examined the horses and mules for any signs of wounds. As they made their way out of town, the townspeople stood off the road in small groups; although they heard mutterings, no one tried to stop them. Once out of Vezelay, they traveled in quiet and darkness for several hours before Bertrand moved up beside William and said quietly, "I think we need to call for a halt. I don't think they'll follow us tonight. We need food and sleep and maybe even some talk."

William said in a small voice, "Yes, you're right." Then, he stopped his horse and told the band that they were making camp for the night.

They prepared a quick, dull meal of trail stew over a small, cheerless fire. No one spoke while they ate. As Louis and Odo packed away the pots and plates, the rest moved closer to the fire as if to draw comfort from the flames. That is, all except Thomas, who sat with his back to a tree facing away from the fire. William, Henry, Bertrand, and Mary stared at the dancing yellow and orange flames and the blood-red embers, lost in thought. A veil of bewilderment, regret, and anger filled their thoughts and emotions. Louis and Odo soon joined them.

After a few minutes of quiet, Louis could stand it no longer

33

and said, "Why were we attacked? They called us heretics. Did you hear them? Another man said we were the sons of the Devil. Did they mistake us for someone else? I'm no heretic. Sure, I may have missed prayers a few times or bent a few rules of the Order, but nothing important." Thomas made a barely audible grunt from behind the tree.

Not seeming to have noticed, Louis continued, "I'm fairly certain none of us are the offspring of the Devil, not even Sergeant Bertrand."

Bertrand, with as near to a grin as Thomas has ever seen on his face, said, "Young Louis, you may get an argument from the good Father on that."

Thomas stood, turning to face Bertrand, and said, "You should not joke about such things."

Henry glared at the priest and said sharply, "Priest, why were we attacked? They knew we were Templars. You know something, something you haven't told us. Tell the truth, priest, or I'll cut you down where you stand, even if it means I'll suffer an eternity in Hell."

Thomas, outraged and yet frightened, looked to William. But William only looked at the fire as if he hadn't heard. On the other hand, Sergeant Bertrand looked at the priest as if he found this entire exchange quite amusing.

Realizing he was alone, Thomas scowled back at Henry and said, "Watch your tongue. You endanger your soul, even threatening me. God is all-powerful and all-knowing. He hears your very thoughts and even more the vile threats you make against one of His beloved."

Bertrand looked at Thomas and said, "The worst part about you, priest, is that you believe you are more important to God than the rest of us. I hope if there truly is a God, He's not the one you pray to."

Thomas, in an outrage, turned entirely red, raised a finger to point at Bertrand, and spat out, "You are accursed! You evil man. You will surely die in your sin and suffer the torments of Hell! God will spit you out of His mouth, you filthy abomination!"

Far from being shaken by this outburst, Bertrand looked back into the flames dancing on the logs and said, "You're probably right, priest, but if God is really how you describe Him, that's where I'd

34

rather spend eternity. You never answered Sir Henry's question: why were we attacked?"

Still seething in anger, Thomas said, "I'll not answer questions from one such as you." With that, he turned his back on the fire and started to step away from its feeble glow.

Still staring into the fire, William said, "Answer the question, Thomas, or you'll go no further with us."

Thomas turned back to face them and started to give another lashing retort, but seemed to think better of it and said, "I guess it doesn't matter anymore anyway. There have been rumors from individuals who have the Pope's confidence that King Philip has been planning to accuse the Templars of heresy. Part of the plan was to have all members of the Order arrested. It appears the rumors were correct. That is why Grand Master de Moley had me come along. I have been trained in ecclesiastical law, and he thought if we ran afoul of the local officials, I might be able to keep us on the mission. However, it has obviously progressed beyond what my words can help. I believe we should turn ourselves in at the next House of God we find and trust in the wisdom of the Church before we are attacked again."

There was stunned disbelief among the group. The long silence was broken by deep, booming laughter. Sergeant Bertrand was nearly doubled over in hysterics. Louis placed a hand on Bertrand's shoulder and said, "I don't think he's joking."

Bertrand looked up, wiping tears from his eyes, and said, "Neither do I, young man. I am surprised it took this long for pretty King Philip and his puppet Pope to act."

"You knew they had this planned?" William asked the Sergeant in disbelief.

Bertrand shook his head and said, "No, but I know King Philip has nearly emptied France's coffers in fighting England. Like many others, he believes that we Templars have a fortune stashed at every commandery and outpost. I also know all of Christendom wants someone to blame for the loss of the Holy Lands, and following our defeat at Ruad, we are a perfect choice. Suppose the Pope can show that Jerusalem was lost because Templars are in league with the Muslims or Satan or, better still, both. In that case, Rome won't appear wrong in calling for the Crusades in the first place."

Henry asked, "Even if it is true, why would a seneschal in this out-of-the-way town bother to try and arrest us? We're not important. Wouldn't they just arrest the leaders of the Order?"

After a moment, Bertrand answered, "No, they would need to arrest us all, or at least as many as they can. If they just arrested the leaders of the Order, they would be leaving the best-trained army in France free to demand the release of those imprisoned. If they have us all locked away, no one will interfere with whatever propaganda they decide to spread. Actually, this may be even worse. Priest, what else do you know? What of our brothers in England, Spain, and elsewhere?"

Thomas considered momentarily, telling them he knew nothing more than what he had already told them. Then, he decided that a little truth would make it easier to continue with his mission. "I know that if the Church believes the Order to be corrupt enough to arrest Templars here, they will want the Templars arrested everywhere. And I know that King Philip has made his accusations against the Order known to the monarchs in other countries where commanderies are located."

"How could you possibly know that?" asked Louis

"Well, to say I 'know' might be a little strong, but the Grand Master did communicate his fears to me. I'm sure you know that many monarchs feel there is little need for the Templars. They do not like or want a standing army in their kingdoms that is not under their control. The other Orders have had the wisdom to take on additional tasks since the loss of the Holy Lands. But you Templars are seen as a threat to the stability of the various monarchies. Many Templars are viewed as arrogant drunkards by the people where commanderies exist. Most damning though is that there have been rumors of secret meetings and rituals that are unholy, taking place in the Templar commanderies, which reputedly are used to initiate knights and sergeants into an evil pact with the Devil."

Louis said, "What do you mean by 'You Templars?' Aren't you a Templar, Father?"

Father Thomas merely looked at Louis with revulsion and said nothing.

Sir Henry said, "We had best assume we are on our own. We may find no help from our brother Templars or from our mother Church. We will have to save ourselves."

36

Thomas commented out of habit, "There is no salvation except through the Church."

Sergeant Bertrand flared at the priest, "I, for one, would be happy to have broken ties with the Church. It was in the name of Rome that we slaughtered innocent women and children in Outremer. Most of the large-scale atrocities took place before I got there, but there were plenty of brutalities done in the name of the Church for me to experience. Why, priest, do we have to kill everyone who disagrees with Rome?"

"The only way to Heaven is through the Church. Those who reject that should, at first, be made aware of their error in an attempt to bring them into the fold of Christ's compassion. If they continue to refuse the Love of God, then the best choice is to kill them for their continued opposition to God and the Church. Otherwise, the darkness in their soul will spread to others that they may influence, condemning more people to an eternity in hell. Better for one infidel to die at two years old than to allow him to live to forty and drag hundreds more off to Hell with him," replied Thomas.

"You weren't there, or you would not speak so blithely of killing children," Bertrand said quietly as he stood and moved into the dark, away from the group.

Mary spoke for the first time that evening, "I don't understand. The Church talks of love and compassion, but seems to abandon so many people. It seems the Church always wants us to give more money, even though we have little or none. At the same time, the Church does little to help the poor; although the Church may assist a few people, it appears that the masses continue to live in poverty while the Church becomes increasingly wealthy. We are promised eternal life if we obey the Church, the Lord of the lands we inhabit, and anyone else in a higher station than us. Yet many of those over us treat the poor almost like slaves and then cast us off as chattel when we have legitimate needs. Why doesn't the Church do something to help us? We often starve all winter and slave away in the fields the rest of the year. Many children die in their first year, and nearly as many mothers die while giving birth. But all we are told is to have faith, give more, submit to authority, and God will reward you."

Thomas responded in a condescending tone, "The Church offers the wretched poor the only happiness they are likely ever to

37

see: happiness in the hereafter, in Heaven. Even when we offer this eternal gift, we are perceived as money-grubbers because we ask for a tithe to help cover the expenses of our consecrated calling. The Scripture tells us a workman is worthy of his hire."

William, somewhat shocked at this response, said, "I thought the Church was supposed to help the poor. You can do nothing for them here in this life?"

Thomas said, "It is the Church, not the soldiers or even the Kings, that keeps the peace. Do you think the peasantry would stand for their low lot in life if it were not for the promised gift of Heaven if they do as they are told? You would have no grain to feed those fine horses you ride, no food on your table, and no chainmail on your back if the poor were not used as they are. There will always be the poor among us, and we can either give them a purpose that will aid society or allow them to revolt and destroy society. The only thing that keeps them from drifting into rebellion is the hand of the Church and the promise we offer of everlasting life in Heaven. Without us, this country would come to a halt in a matter of weeks, and anarchy would rule. We keep the peace with the cross, not you soldiers with the sword. That is why we believe, because without belief in Heaven, what purpose would there be in life?"

Louis said, with sadness in his voice, "Is that why you believe, because not believing leaves your life empty?"

Thomas visibly flared with anger, but unsure how to respond to that comment, he walked to where he was going to sleep and lay down with his back to Henry and the rest. Slowly, they all moved to their blankets and, without another word, drifted off to sleep. All except Sergeant Bertrand, who sat in the darkness a few feet from the rest, keeping watch. He alone seemed to realize they were in enemy territory and knew it was necessary to place a guard. The rest of the party did not even consider that they could be ambushed while they slept. And besides, he didn't want to sleep. He was afraid to sleep.

Chapter 7

1291

"Sergeant Bertrand, you listen to me. You are to lead these soldiers of Christ to Safita and allow them to complete the mission the Church has sent them here to accomplish."

"What mission? There's nothing in Safita but women and children. There are no Mamelukes soldiers there!"

Sir Gerald glared at his disobedient sergeant for a moment, then said in a hissing voice, "Those women and children are just as cursed by the Church as the warriors. You lead these warriors for the Holy Church there. You allow these new recruits from France to kill the infidel so that they can win a place in Heaven and go home and tell others how important the work we Templars are doing here in Outremer is. These men are not adequately trained to fight skilled soldiers. Still, they can serve the greater cause by improving our image back home so that we can get the support to mount a new crusade and win back the Holy Lands for good. What do you care about a few Muslims anyhow?"

Bertrand said, "I don't care about the Muslims: men, women, or children. I'm just sick of all the killing of harmless people. This is not why I became a Templar. I thought we were to protect travelers from war parties or cutthroats and retake the Kingdom of Jerusalem from enemy soldiers." Then, after a pause and a sigh, Sergeant Bertrand continued, "I'll take this band of ruffians on this little trip, but only because you are ordering me to. I'll point them at the undefended, helpless town, but I see no point."

"You don't need to see a point. That's not your station in life."

On June 12, 1291, Sergeant Bertrand led a contingent of around 130 poorly armed and ill-trained men of dubious character out of Tortosa, one of a handful of Christian strongholds left in the Holy Lands. Sidon, Tortosa, and Athlit were the only castles left to the Templars. The Templars did not have enough men to attack the Mamelukes led by Shunjai and al-Ashraf. They simply waited behind their walls for the enemy to come to them; it would not be a long wait.

Sergeant Bertrand did not enter Safita with the rabble he led

39

there. He chose to sit outside the city and wait for the murder, rape, and pillaging to end. It was late afternoon. He would sleep outside the city, then go in at first light and begin the laborious task of rousing the men he could find and head back to Tortosa. As he gathered wood for a fire, Bertrand could hear the cries from inside the city. There were few men there, no soldiers, mostly women and children. The lucky ones successfully hid from the depraved actions of these men who acted under what they believed to be the protection of the Church in Rome and the Will of God. Bertrand led the men to the town at a slow pace, hoping word would travel ahead of them and give much of its helpless population time to evacuate and hide. It appeared many remained. Bertrand attempted to ignore the cries. The pleas for help or mercy he had heard all too many times. Appeals that went unheeded by man or whatever God they were directed at.

Suddenly, a woman and a small boy of two or three burst forth out of the brush. The woman did not see Bertrand until that moment. She froze, holding the child close to her chest, and looked behind her just as one of the men Bertrand had led to Safita crashed out of the same bush.

The man grinned at Bertrand and said, "Thanks Sarg, I don't think I could have caught the fleet-footed bitch even though she carried the whelp."

Bertrand noticed the smell of fear coming from the woman and heard the terrified whimpers from the small boy. He told the man, "Go back to the city. Leave these to me."

"I would, Sarg, but I've taken a fancy to this bitch, and her boy might do as a snack after I've had my fun with her and slit her throat."

"I said, leave them and go back!" Bertrand bellowed

At this, the man lunged forward. With a single thrust of his sword, he plunged it first through the mother, then the son. "If I can't fuck them, at least I can kill them."

Bertrand saw in slow motion the life slip from the mother as he gazed helplessly at her. Then he saw only red, not blood, but red of blind, furious anger. Before he thought about what he was doing, he had drawn his sword and lopped off the man's head in a violent, savage rage.

That night, he decided to leave the Holy Lands and the Order

40

of the Knights Templar. He rode his horse through the dark desert night back toward Tortosa. He abandoned "his men" in Safita. He no longer cared about a duty to an organization for which he had lost all respect. The Templars were founded with a noble cause: to protect defenseless pilgrims in the Holy Land after the success of the First Crusade. The Order grew from humble beginnings: nine knights led by Hugh de Payn. These knights took monastic vows of poverty, chastity, and obedience. They were committed to living their lives by The Rule, which was written to control all aspects of their life as warrior monks. It seemed the Order may have died away, for as near as anyone can tell, no one else joined the Order for almost nine years. Then suddenly, the Order rose practically overnight to unprecedented power and influence. Lands were given to them, and men flocked to join the new Order. Some attribute this growth to the involvement of Bernard of Clairvaux (later canonized Saint Bernard), a staunch supporter of the new Order. However, there have also been rumors that the original nine knights uncovered something of great value and influence when they established their home on the site given to them by Baldwin II, King of Jerusalem.

The site designated as their headquarters in Jerusalem was a section of the al-Aqsa Mosque on the Temple Mount, a building believed to have been constructed on the site of the original Temple of Solomon. Many believed these nine knights uncovered the Ark of the Covenant, the Spear of Destiny, the Holy Grail, or any of a hundred other items of reputed power.

Whatever the cause for growth, the Templars became a power to challenge that of even the great countries of Europe. They had a large fleet that sailed throughout Europe and the Middle East, and some claim that the fleet sailed their ships to lands unknown to the Christian world. Their soldiers were highly trained, and unlike the vast majority of knights in Europe, the Templars knew how to fight as a cohesive unit. They had the protection of the Church in Rome, should any king try to interfere with them. They were exempt from all taxes since they were a religious order. This, combined with their strong work ethic, allowed them to accumulate great wealth and power.

None could deny they had secrets. They developed a secret code that allowed them to become Europe's first true banking system. For a small fee, an individual traveling to the Holy Land

41

could deposit money at the commandery in Paris and receive a note that allowed the Templars in the Holy Land to pay out the money to the individual. These notes had to be in code; otherwise, they could be forged. Therefore, the Templars had to develop a system to protect the code. They were very good at keeping secrets, and this, in part, would lead to their destruction.

As time passed and the Holy Lands were slowly lost, the Order seemed to lose its original purpose. In addition, as any organization grows in size, wealth, and influence, it inevitably develops its share of controversy and conspiracy theories. Many thought that they were becoming more of a problem than a help. It was believed in some circles that it was time for the Templars to be dissolved. And some greedy men saw an opportunity to take back lands given to the Order, lands they could then tax. And there was the wealth that everyone "knew" the Templars had hidden away. Many believed there was something else, an object or a secret that, if discovered, would provide great power or shake the foundations of power that currently existed. But no one dared move against the mighty Templars with their huge, well-trained army, fast-moving fleet, and the protection of Rome, at least not in 1291.

By the time the sun had risen, Bertrand was almost at the walls of Tortosa. He had little idea of what he would say to his commander. Bertrand planned to go to Sir Gerald to return the horse and other Templar possessions "loaned" to him and inform him of his intentions to leave the Order and return to France. However, upon his arrival at the commandery, he found that Gerald had been recalled to France and that a new man, Sir Jacques de Molay, now oversaw Tortosa.

Jacques de Molay listened without comment as Bertrand bared his soul to him about the events of the previous day. At the end of Bertrand's explanation, Jacques de Molay merely said, "I do not give you leave to return to France. I am placing you on kitchen duty for leaving the men under your charge in Safita. You will eat off the floor until I see fit to relieve you. But you will stay here under my command." And with that, he dismissed the exhausted and utterly confused Sergeant.

Bertrand was never sure why he stayed on. Perhaps it was that Jacques de Molay sent all non-Templars home, or maybe it was the way he treated everyone fairly, albeit harshly. He seemed to

42

have the honor that Bertrand thought had vanished from the Templars. Whatever the reason, Bertrand stayed.

In August of that year, the Templars left Tortosa and Athlit for good. Bertrand traveled with the rest of the Templars from Tortosa by ship to Cyprus. There, he met the newest Grand Master of the Templars, Theobald Gaudin. Bertrand was not impressed with Gaudin. He didn't know what to do with the army he commanded and floundered any chance of maintaining even a foothold in the Holy Lands. Luckily for the Templars, he was Grand Master for only a brief time. After Gaudin's death, Jacques de Molay became the Grand Master of the Templars, the last Grand Master they would have, although not the last leader.

Bertrand stayed with the new Grand Master upon his return to France. Although Jacques de Molay never confided any of his many secrets to the Sergeant, he was among the few men with whom he would share his heart.

Bertrand learned that Jacques de Molay believed he was called to be the leader of the Templars at this pivotal point in history and felt they were destined for great and mighty things. First and foremost was retaking the Holy Lands and returning to their original commandery on the Temple Mount. Jacques de Molay never told him how they were to accomplish this with little to no help coming from Europe and with all the Knightly Orders (Templars, Hospitallers, Teutonic Knights, etc.) still in Outremer who were fighting amongst one another for the scraps of what was left; however, he often commented that a tremendous change was about to take place and the Templars were going to be at the heart of that change. He also firmly believed that soon Christendom would unite and that a new crusade led by the Templars would then drive the infidel permanently out of the Holy Land.

Although Bertrand believed the Grand Master's passion was honest, he did not have confidence that any grand change was about to happen. That is until the night before he left on this mission, and Jacques de Molay came to his quarters to reveal one of the best-kept secrets in the history of civilization.

Chapter 8

In the morning, it seemed that the entire experience of the previous night was but a dream. The members of the company acted as though nothing had happened the night before. They seemed to be back to their old selves, all except Bertrand and Thomas. These two ignored the rest of the party and quietly went about their private business. Since they were often solitary, no one seemed to notice at first. After a quick breakfast of dried meat, they mounted up and prepared to continue their journey until William observed Bertrand still sitting by the embers of the morning's fire.

William called to him, "Sergeant, the sun's up. It's time to get moving."

Bertrand looked up at William and said, "We need to discuss what we are going to do and exactly how we will continue to fulfill our orders. Although most of you seem inclined to forget about last night, I'm afraid the present situation has changed our travel plans."

William, who very much did not want to discuss what had happened the previous evening, said, "I'm sure last night was of no consequence to our mission. A misguided rabble in an out-of-the-way hamlet. I believe it was all some terrible mistake."

Henry joined in, "Or more likely just an attempt to rob us of what they thought was a great treasure."

This brought a snicker from Louis, who added, "The bust of Jacques De Molay that we carry is surely of great value to someone...somewhere."

Bertrand said, "It was no rabble that directed the attempt to arrest us, although you are correct about the majority of those involved. But I'm afraid things have changed significantly. I think we are now hunted by the Crown of France, our countrymen, and very possibly by the Roman Church."

At this, William got off his horse and approached Bertrand. "It can't be that bad. The Pope would not move against us, and our Grand Master is a personal friend of the King. You are making this into something bigger than it is, probably due to not sleeping well."

"No, I didn't sleep well! I didn't sleep at all! I sat up all night, keeping watch. Something you should have thought about doing since you are supposed to be leading this expedition. But instead, you slept, and when you finally woke, you decided that all you had experienced last night was nothing more than a bad dream. But it really happened! People really died trying to arrest us! And you want to continue as we have, not believing anything has changed. Unless you open your eyes and start to behave like a soldier and accept the leadership role that Grand Master has placed you in, you will lead us all to death… or worse. We need information, and we need a plan!" The tirade took them all by surprise. William was at a total loss: on the one hand, he was hurt by the personal attack on his command ability; on the other, he had to admit that Bertrand spoke truthfully.

Louis, as usual, broke the stunned silence: "I guess Odo and I might as well get the fire built up and maybe go hunt up a little fresh meat while the rest of you decide what to do." He climbed down from the wagon and began looking for his bow.

Without taking his eyes off Bertrand, William said, "No, Louis. If the sergeant is correct, I'm afraid that the decisions we are about to make will require Odo and your input as well. I don't think we can afford to think of you and Odo as servants any longer. As much as I hate to admit it, Sergeant Bertrand is right; I was not behaving as I should have. We are possibly in serious trouble here in our own country. We will likely need all our swords and should listen to everyone's counsel. Sergeant, do you think we will be safe here while we make our plans?"

Bertrand replied, "For the present, I think we are as safe here as anywhere." The others slowly dismounted their horses or climbed from the wagon. The high-spirited air had withdrawn, and in its place, the group now appeared despondent. They all sank to the ground as though they were bone weary. Even Louis was subdued.

Bertrand broke the unnatural silence by saying, "I believe that the King's men are seeking us Templars. I believe King Philip has decided he wants our wealth, lands, and establishments and means to have them by destroying our brotherhood on the grounds of heresy."

Henry said, "Heresy? How can he charge us with heresy? He's not the Pope. The King has no authority over us. And the charge is laughable. How could anyone possibly believe we're heretics?"

Bertrand replied, "This is not the first time a group has been targeted by a King of France or a Pope when they saw a need to

45

work together. Recall the Albigensian Crusade in Southern France against the Cathars in Languedoc. The Cathars were also accused of heresy and destroyed or at least suppressed to the point of not being a perceived threat to the Church or the Crown. In Beziers, close to where we are heading, when neither Catholics nor Cathars would come out of the city as ordered, the Catholic army killed the entire population. When the papal legate was asked how to distinguish Catholic from Cathar before the slaughter began, he told the military commander, "Kill them all! God will know his own." When a King or Pope sees a threat or an opportunity, they act to serve what they feel is the best interest of their Kingdom. Whether it be France or the Kingdom of Heaven, they do not pay much attention to individuals or the truth. King Philip may not be the Pope, but he has the Pope held on French soil with or without his consent, I do not know. I do know that Pope Clement does not appear to have much of a backbone."

"Blasphemy!" Thomas nearly shrieked. "You would speak ill of the man chosen by God to lead His Church here on Earth? You are a fool and a damned fool at that! And this brute (he pointed his long, thin finger at Sir Henry) thinks it not possible anyone would believe charges of heresy. There are meetings held in the dead of night, secret rites, sacred items that none but the leaders in the Order know anything about, and they deny their existence when confronted by the Church. Even the money handlers within the Templars have a secret code they use for transactions. And all these secrets are kept even from us priests within the Order. It is a small wonder heresy hasn't been charged before."

William said, somewhat sardonically, "I sense a tone of resentment in your voice. I believe you were aware that we were a military order when you joined the Templars. As a military Order, there is going to be a certain amount of secrecy kept even from those within the Order who do not need to be aware of certain information. And again, Father Thomas, you seem more knowledgeable regarding these events than the rest of us."

Thomas said, "I know no more about what is going on than what I told you last night." With that, Thomas stood and left the group.

Odo said in a hushed voice, "Father Thomas is correct that we do not know enough. We need information in order to form a

46

plan."

Louis said, "Maybe we should return to Paris and speak with the Grand Master."

William shook his head, "I have orders to take this wagon to Rennes-le-Chateau. We cannot turn around."

Bertrand said, "Maybe we should send one or two back to Paris. If we all go in disguise, some of us can travel north back to Paris on the main roads while the rest continue to travel south along lesser-traveled byways. Those traveling to Paris without the wagon and on better roads can travel much faster. They can find out what is going on and then return. We can meet up again in Toulouse at the first pub along the north-south road. That way, we may know something before we walk into Rennes-le-Chateau with this cargo."

"I'll return to Paris," Henry said. "Odo and I will. But not in disguise. I am a Templar, and anyone who tries to arrest me for that will learn what sword skills I have."

"You arrogant piss-ant," said Bertrand. "This is not only about you! We need information. Not a hero with something to prove."

Trying to head off an angry retort from Henry, William said, "I don't want to split up our swords. There are not many to begin with. But I suppose we do need information. And it seems either Sir Henry or I must go back to Paris... I don't like this... I cannot leave the wagon; the order was given to me. Henry, as you said, you and Odo will return to Paris. You should take Father Thomas with you as he will only slow us down traveling cross-country."

"I will go with them back to Paris," said Mary.
William merely nodded to Mary, indicating that her return to Paris was fine with him.

Louis said, "Do you think that's a good idea? Shouldn't she stay with the rest of us? Paris may not be safe."

William said, "No, she should return to Paris. We may be traveling through some rough country, and having a woman traveling with them may help to hide the fact that they are Templars. Speaking of hiding, I think we should all shave our beards. They are not the fashion except in our Order and are sure to give us away."

Bertrand added, "And the sooner, the better. Our faces will be much lighter where our beards are until the sun browns them a bit. I've had this beard for so many years. It'll be like losing a

47

friend."

Henry said, "You want me to shave my beard, too? I don't like skulking around. We have done nothing. Hiding only makes us look guilty."

William said, "Speed is of the essence. If Thomas and the Sergeant are correct, Templars are being sought after by the authorities. The only way to move quickly is in disguise."

Henry looked as though he was going to reply, but instead shrugged his shoulders.

The conversation was over, water was boiled, and the men shaved their facial hair; Henry and Bertrand chose to keep their mustaches. Surcoats with the distinctive Templar cross were removed and hidden among riding kits. Likewise, the Templar cross on Henry, William, and Sergeant Bertrand's shields was covered by attaching a plain leather cover over the face of the shield. The leather was taken from riding cloaks. Henry was not pleased with the idea of hiding who he was. Still, he did have to admit that he would have a much better chance of reaching Grand Master Jacques de Molay more quickly if he rode in this disguise.

Farewells were said, and the party split into two groups. To William's surprise, Thomas never said a word but merely left with the Paris-bound group. William did notice the hurt expression on Louis' face as he watched Mary seated on one of the extra riding horses, talking to Odo without looking back at Louis.

It was late morning by the time William, Bertrand, and Louis started toward Rennes-le-Chateau. No one spoke as the wagon creaked along the dirt road. William's mind once more wandered to what was in the wagon and this mysterious mission. Was he right to divide the members of his already small band? Although Henry de Creon was a skilled swordsman, he had little real experience, only extensive practice. William was certain that Henry's first real fight had been yesterday, like himself. William also worried about Henry's temper: could he keep his mouth shut long enough to keep them from being found out? Perhaps with a priest and a woman along, no one would challenge him. Henry was beyond his control now. William could only hope and pray he'd done what was best for his mission.

Bertrand's mind turned to his parting words with Jacques de Molay. Perhaps he should talk to William and let him know what the Grand Master had confided in him, but would that really change anything? They would still have the same mission to carry out, and the precautions they had taken were as many as they could do. The only other option that came to mind was to hide the wagon and its contents in a secure location, allowing them to make better time to Rennes-le-Chateau and obtain additional help from the villagers to guard the wagon adequately. But Bertrand knew William would never leave the wagon and its contents behind. William de Sevrey has a family tradition to live up to.

1291

After the Latin armies retook Acre during the Third Crusade, it became the base of operation for the Christian soldiers. With the fall of Tripoli in 1289, Acre was the only city of any size that the Christians held in the Kingdom of Jerusalem. The city was protected by two lines of thick walls and twelve towers. It was open to the sea, facilitating resupply and reinforcement.

On April 5, 1291, a massive Muslim army led by al-Ashraf Khalil began the siege of Acre. The city's defenders included armies from the Hospitallers, the Teutonic Knights, and the Templars. Envoys had been sent for reinforcements to the Christian rulers, but little help had arrived. After several days of skirmishing, Khali's numerically superior army had moved barricades close enough to the walls so that they could begin mining under the towers. Trebuchets kept up a constant bombardment that steadily damaged the defensive walls around the city. The Christian army realized they did not have the strength to hold off the sizeable Muslim force, even with the reinforcements from Cyprus that began to trickle in. On May 5th, hope was restored when Henry II, King of Cyprus, arrived with forty ships containing his knights and soldiers.

On May 8th, the towers began to fall due to the bombardment and the work of the miners, who began to collapse the tunnels they had dug. A few days later, al-Ashraf Khalil ordered an all-out attack, which nearly completed the fall of Acre, but when night came and darkness fell, the Muslim army retreated. During the night, Henry II, along with all his knights and soldiers, reboarded their ships and left the city to its fate.

In the morning, the attack resumed with the addition of the Muslim cavalry, who rode over the defensive ditch on the bodies of

49

Khalil's servants, who willingly threw themselves in the ditch to make a bridge with their bodies. The Hospitallers decided any further resistance was futile, so they boarded their galleys and left Acre. The Master of the Templars was killed in the street fighting after a javelin struck him under the left armpit following the breaching of the walls. Those of the inhabitants and defenders of Acre who could escape to the north corner of the city took refuge behind the walls of the Templar fortress.

Peter de Sevrey was now in charge of what remained of the defenders, along with a large number of women and children who sought refuge within the Templars' fortress. After five days of holding out against his army, al-Ashraf Khalil sent an envoy to Peter de Sevrey, who now commanded the remaining resistance. He stated that if Peter surrendered the fortress, the Templars could keep their weapons and possessions, take the women and children who had sought safety with the Templars, and leave the city. Peter agreed, believing it was the only way to protect the women and children under his care.

Approximately 100 Mamelukes entered the fortress to oversee the surrender. The Mamelukes began to abuse the women and young boys sexually. At the sight of this, the Templars drew their weapons and killed the Mamelukes. Before the sultan's army could react, the Templars closed the gates and shouted that the fight was to the death. Knowing there was little time left, Peter de Sevrey had Theobald Gaudin, the Treasurer of the Knights Templar, and as many women and children as they could board a Venetian ship and depart for Sidon. It is believed that Theobald also carried with him an object of great value to the Templars when he escaped.

The next morning, the Sultan apologized for his men's actions on the previous day. He requested that Peter de Sevrey come out of the fortress so that he could apologize in person. Peter, with a small contingent of Templars, left the safety of the fortress to meet the al-Ashraf Khalil. But as soon as they were outside the walls, they were forced to their knees and beheaded. The fortress itself was soon destroyed, and everyone in it was killed when the miners collapsed the tunnels that they had dug under its foundation.

After he escaped to Sidon, Theobald Gaudin was soon elected the next Grand Master of the Knights Templar. He only commanded for about a year, and he died in 1292. Jacques de

Molay was elected the twenty-third and final Grand Master of the Knights Templar.

Chapter 9

Henry de Creon, Odo, Mary, and Father Thomas made good time. The one obstruction to their rapid progress was when they had to leave the main road to avoid the town of Vezelay. The only conversation beyond the few words necessary was between Odo and Mary. Even though Henry was steaming over having to hide being a Templar, he did find a certain amount of amusement and was oddly warmed by the change in Odo. Odo rarely spoke to anyone; he was shy, quiet, and hard-working. He was what Henry felt the perfect squire should be. But after the first few hours of Mary talking with Odo, trying to draw him out, Odo began speaking in reply to Mary's many questions. At first, just one-word responses, and then more conversational. To Henry's surprise, he began to hear some inflection in Odo's usually monotone voice. Henry was positive that he saw Odo smile at least once.

At dusk, seven days after splitting up, they re-entered Paris. They wound their way through the street toward the Templar commandery, and for the first time in several days, Henry began to feel his old self again. He believed that as soon as he reached the commandery, everything would be explained and that he would be back within the brotherhood of Templars. Although Henry often resented what he perceived as the false piety of the Templars over the years, he had grown to love their camaraderie. The simple discipline and hard training of the Knights Templar were also strangely satisfying. There was pure comfort in being a part of such a group of warriors. These were the thoughts that occupied Sir Henry de Creon as they rode up to the Paris commandery. Too late, he noticed that the soldiers out front of the gate were not Templars but knights and footmen of King Philip.

Henry, leading his small group, started to turn his horse down a side street when one of the King's knights called out, "Hold, Sir Knight! What is your name, and what is your business here?"

Henry turned his horse to face the knight who was walking toward him, flanked by half a dozen other soldiers, all on foot. "I am traveling through this part of the city on my way to my father's house in the northern section of Paris."

"And who might your father be, Sir Knight?" asked the spokesman.

Henry responded with all the haughtiness he could manage to convey in a tone of voice, "I don't see what concern it is of yours, but in the hopes that it will satisfy your unquenchable curiosity, my father is Robert Duke of Creon." Henry's tone of voice and his father's title had the desired effect.

The King's knight said, "I apologize if I have appeared overzealous, but I cannot be too cautious given the situation we face."

Henry leaned forward in his saddle and said, "I have just returned to Paris after being in Burgundy, looking in on my father's farms and vineyards there. What is this crisis that has so inflamed you that you would stop and molest a member of the chivalry in this manner?"

The King's knight seemed to relax a bit and smiled the grin of a man who has the pleasure of revealing a great and dark secret. "You must have come by backroads all the way. It was discovered by King Philip and his advisor, Guillaume de Nogaret, that the Knights Templar are heretics, worshipers of Satan hiding among us. On October 13th, King Philip ordered the arrest of all the Templars in France."

"Heretics! What insanity is this? The Templars?! They held the Holy Lands and kept them safe while the rest of Christendom went back home. And now they're heretics?!" Henry's anger exploded in such a tirade that Odo and Mary were sure it would give them away.

The King's knight didn't seem at all suspicious. He responded in a conciliatory tone, "I know. I felt the same way when I first heard, but there are many confessions of evil deeds from the Templars themselves that prove their guilt."

"Confessions? Who has confessed?" Henry demanded.

"A number of the knights and brothers have confessed to the foulest of crimes: spitting on the cross, worshiping idols, unholy rites carried out in secret nighttime meetings, and homosexual acts."

Henry seemed at a loss for anything to say, and his brain got the better of his tongue for once: "Well, I find this hard to believe, but it's none of my concern. If I have your leave, I will depart for my father's home." And he turned his horse back toward the side street.

Then Henry heard Thomas's voice, like a midnight wind in a

cemetery that blows ice into the heart. "Hold, Knight Templar. Will you continue to deny what you are, like the craven cowards your Order has become?"

This outburst caught everyone by surprise. The King's men were unsure they had heard correctly, and briefly, they froze in indecision. Henry, Odo, and Mary listened to these words of treachery as if out of a nightmare. Henry was the first to react. He drew his sword and charged at Thomas with hot-blooded fury in his eyes. The problem was that he was on a narrow street, and Odo and Mary were between him and Thomas. By the time Henry had pushed aside Mary's horse, one of the King's knights had hooked Henry with the axe-head on his halberd and pulled him backward out of the saddle. Henry rapidly rose to his feet and completely ignored the King's men. His blood was up, and his only thought was to kill Thomas, the priest. Henry charged straight at Thomas, sword drawn and raised, ready to strike. One of the knights struck a hard blow to the back of Henry's head with the butt end of his halberd just as Henry was about to remove Thomas' head. Henry collapsed to the street in a heap.

More knights charged toward them. Odo looked at Mary and said, "Go!" and slapped her horse's flanks as he shifted his horse sideways to block anyone from pursuing her. The next moment, he was roughly pulled from his horse and knocked senseless by a blow from the pommel of a sword.

Thomas, still on horseback, watched the fleeing form of Mary turn her horse down a side street. He said, with great indignation, "Go after her, you fools, she's getting away."

The knight who seemed to be in charge was checking to make sure Henry and Odo were still alive. He looked up at Thomas as the clatter of hoof falls faded to nothingness and said, "I don't care about a Templar's whore. But Templar soldiers, scribes, and priests... these I am to arrest." With that said, he reached up and grabbed the reins of Thomas's horse. Another knight removed him from his saddle and deposited him on the street next to the unconscious Odo and Henry.

Thomas immediately started to stand and said in the loud, commanding voice he used when correcting the young squires, "You don't seem to know who you are dealing with. I demand to see Guillaume de Nogaret immediately."

54

The knight, without a glance at Thomas, said to the soldier standing over the three prisoners, "If that man speaks again, shut him up, but try not to kill him. The King wants as many Templars as possible alive… at least for now."

Chapter 10

Sir Henry de Creon, Knight Templar and son of the Duke of Creon, slowly opened his eyes. He was in a dark, dank place. The odor that assailed his nose was like nothing he had ever experienced before. Feces and urine were major components, but were mixed with the smell of sweat and fear. The air was humid with the moisture of unwashed bodies. At first, Henry thought the room was small. But, as his senses started coming out of the fog caused by the blow to his head, he realized it was a large room filled with many people. Some were murmuring, and others were moaning as if in pain.

Suddenly, he recalled what had happened before he was struck unconscious. He sat up rapidly and was about to stand up, but a hand grabbed his shoulder and restrained him.

"Careful there. The ceilings in this part of the cell are only four feet above the floor. If you must get to your feet, you'll have to stay bent over. You're Sir Henry, correct?"

Still somewhat foggy, Henry said, "Yes, I'm Henry. Where am I? What is this place?"

"Sir Henry, you are a guest of King Philip of France. These luxurious accommodations have been specially prepared for all of us who are members of the Knights Templar. I am Sir Stephen de Albi. We have met a few times, although you may not remember me. The last time we met, you knocked my practice sword from my hand in a backhand slash that ended by striking me along the back. I used to consider myself handy with a sword, but you humbled me rather quickly."

Henry, not really listening, said, "Am I to understand that somehow the poorly trained soldiers of the King have been able to arrest the best-trained soldiers in France? Was he aided by the damned Knights Hospitaller?"

"The Hospitallers played no part in it that I am aware of. The King's men took us without a fight. As far as we have heard, all Templars in France who could be located were arrested on Friday, October 13th, at dawn; you are the only new arrival since we were all brought here," Stephen replied.

"Without a fight?!" Henry roared so loud that several prisoners cringed as men broken by terror would do. "Why did no one fight?"

"I don't know about other locations, but at the Paris commandry, we were ordered by Grand Master Jacques de Molay to put up no resistance. He told us that this would be cleared up shortly, that the King has no official authority over us, and that our Holy Father, the Pope, would soon force our release. It's been over a week since we were thrown in here, as near as I can tell. I guess the Pope is busy."

Suddenly, Henry remembered Odo, Mary, and Thomas. "You said I was the only one brought in here. What about my traveling companions? My squire, a woman, and a priest."

Before Sir Stephen could answer, the gate to the cell opened, and several men entered. Four of the men were dressed in brown robes of the clergy, five were soldiers carrying torches and clubs, but no swords. It was the last eight men who occupied the attention and terror of the inmates. These men carried in several devilish instruments: instruments that brought silent screams to the minds of many and audible, insane sounds to the throats of others.

Chapter 11

Odo found himself in slightly better surroundings than Sir Henry awoke to. He drifted back to the conscious world to find himself in the large dining room and meeting hall of the Templar commandry. Although at first sight, Odo barely recognized it. The room was filthy and smelled worse than any stables he had ever been in. It was also packed with human beings. Most wore the plain tunic that was the standard wardrobe of the squires and servants who labored here, but the clothes had apparently not been changed in several days. After some milling about, Odo found one of the squires he knew.

"Anthony, what's going on?"

"Odo, where did you come from? I thought you left with Sir William."

"I did, but some of us returned to find out what was going on."

Anthony looked at his feet and said, "You should have stayed gone. Everything is wrong. The King's men took all the knights, sergeants, and priests to the King's dungeons. There was no room for us, so we've been left here under guard. We are not allowed to leave this room for any reason. We've agreed to use the room's northeast corner if you must relieve yourself. We get some water and food, but it's horrible and not enough for us all."

Odo said, "Why is this happening? What has the King arrested us for, and why is the Holy Father allowing it to happen?"

"I don't know for sure, but they say that the knights and priests were involved in devil worship and unholy and indecent acts. They say many have already confessed; some have whispered that even the Grand Master has confessed. But I don't believe it," Anthony said somewhat conspiratorially.

Odo, to his surprise, flared with anger. Sure, he had been angry in the past, but it never overpowered his sense of control. Before he could stop himself, he said in a loud, irritated voice, "This is ridiculous. You know the knights and sergeants who served here. Some may have drunk too much wine too often or been too proud of their status, but they are mostly good, honest, brave, and devout men. How can the King hold us here?"

Anthony glanced around in palpable fear, then said in hushed tones, "Odo, lower your voice. They have not questioned us here. But we hear that the knights, sergeants, and priests are being tortured, that the inquisition is soon to come, and then we all must give an account. Look, Odo, you know as well as I do that meetings are held secretly at night with a guard posted who has his sword drawn and ready. Why at night? Why secretly? Maybe the charges are correct. I don't know, one way or the other. I do know that I'm not going to be tortured to keep secrets I know nothing about. I'll say whatever it takes to get out of here, and you should, too. What will it hurt? We don't know anything, really. All we do is practice with sword, lance, and riding for a few hours every day. The rest of our time is spent praying, cleaning rooms, emptying crappers, grooming the horses, keeping the rust off the armor, and doing a thousand other menial tasks; they tell us nothing. I'll not be burned or stretched. I'll say whatever they want to hear, confess to whatever they tell me to, and do whatever penance they give me."

Odo started to respond but realized it was of no use. He just turned his back on Anthony and made his way to the northeast corner of the room, where an intense stench originated.

Chapter 12

Mary fled like a mad animal for several minutes along the nearly deserted and deepening shadows of the streets of nighttime Paris until her horse stumbled and almost sent her to the cobbled road. She reined in the horse and began to walk it as casually as possible. Although Mary repeatedly looked behind her, she saw no sign of pursuit. As the evening wore on, she realized two things: Firstly, no one was looking for her because they must have known she wasn't of any importance; secondly, she was hopelessly lost. It was full dark, and she was a woman alone. She decided she should get out of sight, or some guard might stop her and ask questions she didn't know how to answer. She found a narrow alley behind some merchant shops, hobbled the horse, wrapped the reins around her wrist several times, and tried to sleep sitting against a wall.

Sleep came in short bursts as she constantly awoke due to being uncomfortable and scared. She was up before the sun and brushing the horse. Mary fed the horse a handful of grain she had in her travel supplies. While caring for the horse, she noticed the city began to shudder awake in the predawn darkness. Soon, she could hear voices and the sounds of doors and shutters opening as the sun started to make its presence known. In the early morning light, Mary decided it was finally time for her to try to escape the city. She might have wandered around Paris all day had she not stopped to water her horse at a public cistern. There, a merchant was also watering a team of horses for his wagon. She overheard the merchant tell a woman nearby that he was on his way to Alencon as soon as his horses were watered. Mary decided to fall in behind the wagon, at least until she got out of the city.

It was nearly noon when she finally made it through the city walls. She thanked God she had made it and had not been stopped once. She knew it would not have been so easy if she had been afoot. Being on horseback set her physically above many others and socially above most people in the teeming city, making it less likely that anyone would harass her.

Once outside the city, she had a choice to make. Where should she go? She knew there was no chance of returning to Paris and helping Odo or Henry. Although she had begun to feel an attachment to Odo, it was not of sufficient strength to cause her to behave rashly or foolishly. She realized she had a valuable horse; she could sell it and have enough money to hopefully get somewhere and find honest employment. Or she could try to reach William and the other group, inform them of all that had happened, and hope they could help Odo and Henry. This last choice appealed to her most. It had more focus, and although she only knew that they were on their way to Rennes-le-Chateau, she felt she should try to reach William, Sergeant Bertrand, and Louis.

So, instead of following the merchantman who had unwittingly led her out of the city, she took the southeast road. She hoped she could somehow find her way to Rennes-le-Chateau and the remainder of the band. She would let them know what happened to Odo and Henry. Surely, Sir William or Sergeant Bertrand would know some way to help them. She had no money, but she did have a horse and a few supplies. She believed that by merely being on horseback, she would be safe, at least safer than she would be walking along the roadway by herself.

Chapter 13

Thomas was in one of the small cells of the chapel in the Paris commandery, which they used for visiting clergy. The door had been locked, and he had not been given any water or food. Worse, he had not been allowed to speak to anyone. And his shouts to be given an audience with Guillaume de Nogaret had been ignored.

Thomas, the priest, was more frightened than he had ever been in his life. That was saying a lot, for Thomas lived a life more motivated by fear than any other emotion.

In his childhood, Thomas was constantly bullied by other children. He was raised without a father, the bastard of a whore who showed him little love. At nine years old, his mother left him in their small, rented room one night and never returned. He never knew if something had happened to her or if she had left, not wanting the burden of taking care of him any longer. He waited four days in the hovel until the landlord came to collect rent and found him alone, throwing him out into the streets. He was soon one of the many vermin living in the darkened corners and alleys of the squalid city of Paris. He was much smaller than the other boys and, therefore, was tormented without mercy by them. One cold night, he sought refuge in a church. When the priest found him cowering in a small alcove in the back of the building, he started to toss him out into the street. But, as luck would have it, the Bishop of Toulouse happened to be there. The bishop had a passion for architecture and was in Paris to view its many magnificent buildings.

The bishop stopped the priest. Perhaps he felt compassion for young Thomas, or maybe he saw intelligence in those frightened eyes that no one had yet noticed. The bishop took Thomas with him back to Toulouse and began his education. The bishop was not an affectionate man. He saw to Thomas' needs as far as food and shelter were concerned. His focus was to see Thomas grow spiritually and intellectually. The Bishop had no concern for Thomas' emotional needs. Thomas was still a young boy who desired love and compassion, but he soon learned that these were not things he could receive here. Thomas was also practical and enjoyed learning. While living in the bishopric, he was reasonably warm when it was cold out, and even if he didn't eat well, he did at least eat.

In many ways, Thomas flourished under the tutelage of the bishop. He devoured theology, philosophy, and mathematics and even developed a love for architecture. But in other ways, Thomas also died. His life before coming here had been harsh and likely would have killed him before he reached adulthood, but in that life, his soul had embers of compassion. Those embers began to be extinguished entirely in this wholly academic life.

One afternoon, Thomas had gone to visit the Basilica St-Sernin to sketch its Romanesque architecture. It was dark by the time he was returning to the bishopric, and he happened upon a side street where the prostitutes in the area plied their trade. Thomas, at fourteen years old, was wildly excited and frightened by these bold women who willingly showed their breasts or lifted their skirts to attract a customer. When one of the women reached out and grabbed his arm, he dropped his sketch papers and charcoals and fled to the laughter of everyone who witnessed it.

For the next several months, all Thomas could think about were those prostitutes. Thomas knew he was sinning even to entertain such thoughts, but he couldn't help it. At fourteen, Thomas was motivated by the desire for sex, but he also craved to be held and comforted. Here were women who he could pay to show him attention, which he desired as much as the sexual urge he felt. Thomas longed for a mother who would say she loved him. Deep down, he felt that his mother not only didn't love him but had rejected him. It was all very confusing and frustrating for Thomas.

One night, Thomas could stand it no longer. He knew the bishop kept a "Poor Box" in the waiting room outside his office. If someone wanted to see the bishop to beg for a favor, they knew they must donate to the poor, or they would likely be waiting all day. Thomas also knew that the bishop only emptied the box on Sunday afternoon, and Thomas knew the location of the key. As it was Friday night, Thomas was confident the bishop wouldn't notice if a few coins went missing. He snuck down, got the key, and stole what he hoped were enough coins. He then replaced the key and crept out into the foggy night.

Thomas feared being seen by someone who would recognize him and inform the bishop, but he had already taken the money and knew he would not turn back now. Thomas found the street easy enough and tried to remain inconspicuous as he walked among the prostitutes and their customers. He tried to find one that was young or at least not old, but the light was poor, and the women were all painted up, so it was hard to tell. He noticed one of the prostitutes who appeared younger than most and seemed quieter and less frightening to him. Thomas approached her and held out his hand with the coins, "Is this enough?" he asked timidly.

The woman looked at the coins in his hands and said, "Yes, dearie, that'll do." She scooped up the coins with one hand and took him by the arm with the other. She said as they walked, "For that amount, you get the gentleman's treatment. We'll get off the street and have a go on a bed with mostly clean sheets and all."

She led Thomas down an alley to a small door. She knocked twice, and a large fat man who smelled of fish and sweat opened the door: "Whatcha wants, Gloria? You ain't playing sick on us again, are ya? You gotta make double tonight, or you're out on your ass with no one to protect you, and I get a run at Bridgette."

She dug her fingers into Thomas' arm and pushed past the fat man, dragging Thomas along behind her, and said, "I got double what Jorge wants right here, you mound of shit. Where's Jorge at?"

The fat man never answered as the prostitute yelled, "Jorge, where the fuck is you?"

Thomas grew increasingly alarmed as they made their way through the building. Everything was going wrong: this woman was dragging him somewhere, looking for another man. He didn't understand. Soon, they came to a man sitting behind a small desk wearing an old, slightly soiled suit. He had a scar that ran across his left cheek to his mouth, giving his smile a sinister look. "Why, Gloria. Are we not feeling well today? There's a lot of work to make up for slacking yesterday."

Gloria slammed the coins she had taken from Thomas on the table and said, "There's ya damned money, now let Bridgette out!"

Jorge picked up a coin, examined it, and said, "Is that any way to speak to the man who protects you night and day? And Bridgette is fine. I'd never hurt her. Now, who is this fine young man? I assume he's the one who overpaid for you to spread your legs." Jorge then stood, walked around the table, held out his hand to Thomas, and said, "I'm Jorge."

64

Gloria released her grip on Thomas' arm but glared at him with fury in her eyes. Thomas hesitantly took the offered hand and started to introduce himself when Jorge quickly spun Thomas around and held him tightly against himself, and said, "What shall we do with the horny lad?"

Gloria said, "Slit his throat and throw him in the street. I don't care; just release Bridgette."

Jorge said, "Na, the boy has paid for some fun; we can't disappoint a customer. Let me think. Perhaps Barns would like a go at him. That would make for a story he could tell his friends." Then he yelled, "Barns, you fancy a run at this young boy's ass? I'm sure it's mighty tight right now."

The fat, smelly man stepped into the room and said, "I'm not into boys, Jorge, but I could make an exception for this one."

At that moment, Thomas' bladder let go. Jorge quickly released him and shoved him forward. He stumbled and fell to the floor between Gloria and Barns. Jorge said, "Jeez, kid, we was just messing with you. Get him outta here before he shits himself."

Barns started to reach for him, but Gloria slapped his hand away and said, "I'll see the lad out. You go release Bridgette." Then she grabbed Thomas by the left ear and nearly twisted it off as she forced him to rise to his feet and began directing him out.

As she walked and twisted his ear, she said in a low, angry voice, "Let me educate you, young man. Women don't want your ugly, smelly little cock anywhere near them. They only accept that little worm between your legs so they can survive. That goes for high-born bitches, the same as us whores on the street. They just get paid better for spreading their legs. They get dresses and jewels. The only male a woman can love are their own babies, but once they grow old enough to notice their prick has uses other than pissing, all those messy emotions start to slip away because they know that soon all the boy is going to do is chase after cunts. They learn the little boy is lost to them and will only put up with him if he can give them something they want. You come around here again, and I'll cut that cock off and shove it up your bung hole." And with that, she opened the door and thrust him out onto a dark street.

Thomas ran as fast as his feet would carry him back to the bishopric. He cleaned himself with the water basin in his room as best he could. The next morning, he tried to avoid the bishop as

65

much as possible and attend to his duties. A little after noon, the bishop called Thomas to his office.

As Thomas stood before his desk, the bishop, not looking up from a letter he was writing, said, "Your ear is bleeding, and you smell bad." Thomas chose to remain silent since there was no question in that statement. After a pause, the bishop, still writing, continued, "I noticed the poor box was unlocked this morning. It was locked last night. Any thoughts on how that could have happened?"

"No, your Eminence," Thomas lied.

The bishop scrawled his signature at the bottom of the letter he was writing, then looked up at Thomas. His eyes told Thomas he knew he had lied about the poor box. The bishop said, "I am sending you to the Abbey of Sainte Foy near Conques. You are to walk there barefoot and wear only a rough-spun robe. You are to take enough food for five days, but not to eat any of the food you bring. The food you take is to give to the poor you meet along the way. You are to help anyone you meet in need. Upon arrival, you are to give this parchment to Abbot Renoe; the seal must be intact, or you will not be allowed in the Abbey." The bishop melted some signet wax on the folded sheet of vellum and pressed his seal into the semi-liquid wax. He then handed the letter to Thomas, pulled out a new sheet of vellum, and began to write. He said, "Your robe and the food are waiting for you by the poor box. You are to change and leave immediately. You will take nothing but the food and the letter." And that was the last time Thomas ever heard from or saw the bishop.

Chapter 14

William, Bertrand, and Louis had to stay on the main north-south road for several days, as no minor roads would allow them to travel with the wagon and cargo toward their destination. They saw few others on the road, and none showed any interest in them. The fact that William and Bertrand's shields showed no sign of allegiance probably added to their being left alone. A knight was bad enough, but a knight uncommitted to a Lord was to be avoided by the general populace. These unattached knights were always hungry to prove themselves so that some Lord might take them on as one of his men. They were also often poor and hungry for glory, money, food, and pleasure.

The first few hours after parting from Henry, Thomas, Odo, and Mary, the three companions traveled in relative quiet. Bertrand preferred not to speak unless he had something to say, and William was lost in thoughts of self-recrimination. Louis was still hurt by Mary ignoring him as they parted. But Louis' pain lessened after a while, and ever the optimist, he put the incident behind him. If she preferred Odo, that was fine; Odo was a great guy, a little quiet for Louis' taste, but a great guy. And with that resolved in Louis' mind, he began to talk. Even though William and Bertrand rarely responded, Louis didn't seem to care. He just kept on talking. He talked about life at the commandery, his life before the commandery growing up on a farm in the Champagne district, about what was in the wagon, how bad the mules smelled, how bad he smelled, how they could all use a dip in a pond or river and, wouldn't it be great if they could find a waterfall. He told them all about the time he came across this young lady bathing beneath a waterfall. Come to think of it, she wasn't all that young and was probably no lady, but…and on and on it continued.

They traveled for four days with little contact with anyone. They approached the town of Lyon late in the afternoon on the fifth day. As they rode through the town, Louis suggested they get a few supplies since their diet was "getting quite boring." William, concerned about his charge to get the wagon's contents and the letter safely to Rennes-le-Chateau, was about to tell Louis that they would seek food supplies in a smaller town when Bertrand said, "Good idea. I could use wax to waterproof some of my leather straps before they crack and break anyway."

Louis noticed an inn that served food up ahead and pointed it out. William decided it was not worth quarreling with the two of them, so he agreed.

They left Louis with the wagon, much to his chagrin, while Bertrand and William went in. William began talking with the cook about purchasing some bread, a numble pie, smoked fish, apples, parsnips, mushrooms, leeks, and a couple of candlesticks for the wax. Meanwhile, Sergeant Bertrand went up to the small counter, which served as a bar, and ordered a mug of grog. Already at the counter was a large man who appeared to be a farmer, judging by his appearance and the smell of fresh dirt on him. The farmer, noting that Bertrand was not from Lyons and noticing he wore a sword and armor, said, "Are you here hunting for hidden Templars?" Not appreciating the interruption of his drinking, Bertrand grunted in a non-committal manner. Assuming the grunt was a positive response, the farmer continued, "I say it's about time those Templars got taken down a few notches. First, they take all the donated money, land, horses, and whatever else they claim they need to hold onto the Holy Lands. Then, like cowards, they come running back to France the first time the Muslims shake a sword at them."

Still ignoring the man, Bertrand tried to focus on his drink, hoping the man would take the hint. It didn't work. The farmer, warming to his subject, said in a loud enough voice for everyone in the room to hear, "I hear them Templars were working with the bloody Muslims and were paid by them to leave the Holy Lands. The damned cowards."

William was paying the cook when the farmer made this last comment. William looked at the farmer, fighting the urge to say something, when Sergeant Bertrand decided it was time to respond to the farmer. Bertrand said, "You're right there, friend. I know from experience that the Templars are all money-grubbing cowards." Then he polished off his drink in one last gulp, slapped the farmer on the shoulder slightly harder than was necessary, and walked out the door. William followed with his arms full of supplies. They rode out of town, keeping their eyes on the road directly in front of them, without any further interaction with the people of Lyons.

They never spoke of the incident in the bar. Yet, they both

felt its implications for their future safety. Louis, noticing their quietness, realized that something must have happened. He kept silent until, less than a quarter mile out of Lyons, a bright blue bird flew in front of Louis. Louis responded in his upbeat, excited tone, "I don't believe I've ever seen a bird as blue as that one. Did either of you see him? I once saw a blue jewel in some noble lady's necklace that was the same color, but the jewel was not nearly as bright. I'm sure it's a male since he was so brightly colored. Father Duncan, who taught us squires about animals and plants at the commandery in Paris, told us that male birds had to be more brightly colored to attract female birds. He also informed us that it was the other way around with humans. Women were the ones who prettied themselves up so they could distract men from what was truly important. I don't think he liked women much. I'm not sure he liked anything much. He was always…"

Bertrand rode up beside William and said, "I'd cut your squire's tongue out, but I'm afraid he would just go on talking, and the unintelligible grunting would be even more annoying."

William smiled and, changing the subject, said, "I'm wondering if we shouldn't start heading west."

Bertrand said, "The roads are better if we continue to head south to the coastal road and then turn west."

"I know. However, if we continue south, we will travel close to Avignon, where the Pope resides. I believe we will likely run into the King's men as we get closer. I heard the King has many men-at-arms and knights there to protect the Pope."

Bertrand laughed and said, "Protect the Pope. That's a good one. You mean making sure the Pope doesn't try to escape King Philip and return to Rome."

William stopped his horse and said, "What are you talking about? You make it sound like King Philip is holding the Holy Father captive. A king has no power over the Pope."

Bertrand, who had continued past William, who had suddenly halted. Without looking back, said, "Sir William, I'm sure you are right. Just as I'm sure that all the Arabs are evil, hateful beasts, and all the Christians who want to kill them and take their land are just and righteous."

William, suddenly angry at what he felt was only the latest in a series of disrespectful remarks made at his expense by Bertrand, yelled, "Sergeant-at-Arms, Bertrand, I order you to come back here and speak plainly to me. What are you talking about?"

The outburst caught all three men by surprise. Louis stopped talking mid-sentence, which was highly unusual. William regretted what he had said as soon as the words left his mouth. And Bertrand reined in his horse, turned it about, and walked back to William. He said, "Sir knight, I will speak plainly as you command. The Pope is a captive of King Philip and is not allowed to leave France. Our Pretty King Philip is a vain, evil man with an even more evil advisor in Guillaume de Nogaret. These two men hold the Pope prisoner in Avignon. The Pope may have the power of the Holy See behind him, but he is a weak man. He's afraid of King Philip, and rightly so, for although the King may pretend to be a good Catholic, the only thing he truly holds sacred is himself. Now, am I excused?"

Still ashamed of his outburst, William wanted to apologize, but thought that might appear as a weakness. Besides, why should he apologize? He was a knight and a member of the chivalry, not just a bumbling soldier. So, keeping his face as expressionless as possible, William said, "That may or may not be true. Regardless, I say we take the first road heading west to keep this wagon away from the King's men in Avignon with the Pope." Then, he nodded to Bertrand by way of giving him his leave.

For the rest of the day, Bertrand and William rode in silence. Well, not exactly silence. They didn't speak, but that didn't mean that Louis stopped his one-way conversation. Soon, he was again rambling on about how amazing trees are. "They provided shade, fuel for fire, materials for building houses, barns, fences, and just about everything seemed to be made from trees, even this wagon I'm riding on. And some trees provide us with fruit, although it's not as good as the fruit that grows on a vine. At least not as good as the wine they make from grapes. I could use a nice warm spiced wine about now. I once ran into a guy who told me they could make wine from honey. Has either of you heard of such a thing? That must be some mighty thick wine. You know they make some fine wine back where my home was in Champagne. Once, some monk screwed up a batch by getting bubbles in it, but it turned out that people like bubbles in…"

About two hours before nightfall, they found a road heading west. Bertrand, who was leading the way, dutifully turned his horse onto the road without a word or even glancing back over his shoulder. The road was just wide enough for the wagon. If they encountered another wagon coming from the opposite direction, one of them would have to find a place to get off the road to allow the other to pass. Since the trees surrounding the road were much closer to them, the forest seemed thicker, leaving William feeling as though he was being watched. The fading light of twilight probably increased the ominous feelings. Sergeant Bertrand did not seem to be affected by this feeling. Louis clearly was, for he soon grew silent as if he expected his voice to trigger an attack from the darkening foliage.

Some thirty minutes before dark, Bertrand noticed a level and clear enough place along the roadside where they could park the wagon. He stopped his horse and turned to look at William. He said in a formal, loud voice, "Sir William, if it meets with your pleasure, I believe it would be good to stop here for the night. The squire can prepare the evening meal, and I'll scout ahead a bit to see what lies in front of us."

William, who had again been contemplating how to apologize for his earlier outburst, had his ire reawakened by the Sergeant's tone. He sat up straight in his saddle and just as formally said, "We will do as you suggest, Sergeant." At this, Bertrand wheeled his horse around and trotted down the road without another word.

Louis pulled the wagon off the road in a space between some trees just large enough to accommodate the wagon, mules, and extra horses. He got down and began caring for the animals with William's help. As they finished rubbing down the last of the horses and began to feed each a few handfuls of oats before hobbling and turning them loose to forage for grass, Louis said, "Sir William, I know it's not my place, but don't you think you were a bit harsh with the good Sergeant? I know he's a bit rough, and sometimes it seems he thinks everyone around him is an idiot, but he seems to know what he's talking about. I've never met a man who could make me feel both intimidated and comfortable at the same time. He just seems solid and trustworthy yet still dangerous."

While wiping oat dust from his hands, William said, "You are correct, Louis. It is not your place to discuss matters that are beyond your understanding. Now, get us something to eat while I

71

try and find some water."

Chapter 15

It was long after dark when Mary decided to halt for the night. She had seen no one on the road for the last few hours but feared getting off the horse. As the night grew deeply dark, Mary had trouble making out the road, and she realized she needed to stop for her and the horse's safety. She climbed down and walked him well off into the woods, hoping to stay hidden in the trees away from anyone who might pass by during the night. After rubbing the animal down as Odo had shown her, Mary tied the horse to a tree with enough slack to let him munch grass and hobbled his forelegs. She sat with her back to a tree and ate some of the little rations she had left. Mary began to shiver beneath the rough blanket she had with her, with her few supplies still on the horse. Watching the horse chew grass, Mary wished she could build a fire. But even if she had a flint and steel, she would not risk that the flames might attract intruders.

Although she was near exhaustion from the physical and emotional strain the last 24 hours had put on her, sleep was elusive. Her mind kept presenting all the challenges she faced. The more she thought, the more she doubted her ability to accomplish anything useful to help Odo or Henry. She had no idea where Rennes-le-Château was, only that it was located south.

Mary woke with a start. At some time during the cold night, her fatigued mind must have finally drifted off to sleep. She felt a little better now with the sunlight shining through the trees and the few hours of rest she had gotten. She rose stiffly, sleeping in a sitting position and leaning against a tree had left a chink in her back and neck. She was just beginning to loosen her clenched muscles when she noticed the short piece of rope lying on the forest floor. It was the rope she had used to hobble the horse, and with growing panic, her still-waking mind grasped the fact that the horse was nowhere to be seen.

She began to whistle and turn in circles, calling for him. She started walking through the woods, trying to look in all directions at once. Then, as the consequences of this missing horse began to dawn on her, she started running and calling loudly for the missing animal. As she ran, Mary thought she heard something and turned to the side just in time to miss seeing the branch that caught the side of her head as she ran into it. She fell to the ground in a heap and lay there for some moments in a daze. Her vision cleared, and she slowly got to her feet. She wiped the sweat-streaked grime from her face and looked around, realizing she had no idea in which direction the road was. She cursed herself for being so stupid: first for not tying the horse up well enough and then for getting herself hopelessly lost.

She felt like crying and may have started to, but just then, she heard a sound off to her right. It sounded like an animal or perhaps a person walking in the woods, but was it her horse or something dangerous? She didn't know, but it sounded as though it was walking toward her. Suddenly, she was overcome with fear. She quietly moved to the far side of the tree that had recently knocked her to the ground and peeked around the trunk to see what was coming.

Mary got a glimpse of brown through the leaves, but that told her little. As she watched, a large buck stepped out from behind some trees. Just as it entered a small clearing, he raised his head and looked directly toward her as his ears came forward. The deer's eyes seemed to look into hers as if he was trying to figure out what was peeking out from behind the tree. Then, she heard a twang, and the deer's head suddenly jerked. The deer jumped nearly straight up, took two steps forward, then drunkenly slumped to the ground. It was then that Mary noticed the arrow protruding from the deer's side.

Mary looked off into the woods and saw the hunter. Standing no more than twenty feet away, he wore brown leather clothes and held a long bow in his right hand. The hunter was watching the dying deer but gave her a quick glance, motioning for her to stay where she was and remain quiet. He then went back to watching the deer. While watching the hunter watch the deer, she noticed something was wrong with his face. At first, she couldn't tell what it was, but then she noticed that burn scars were covering one whole side of his face.

After several minutes of silent watching, the hunter quietly crept toward the deer. He had one arrow nocked in the bowstring and held both bow and arrow in one hand. As he got within arm's length of the deer, he reached with his free hand and touched one of the deer's open eyeballs. Seemingly satisfied, he set his bow and

74

arrow aside, drew a large hunting knife, and began the process of field dressing the deer.

The hunter seemed to have forgotten Mary, who stood protectively behind the tree. As she watched him expertly remove the deer's organs, she wondered if she should flee. Was he a threat? She didn't think so. After his brief motion for her to remain still, he seemed oblivious to her presence. She finally decided she might as well ask if he'd seen her horse and, if not, maybe he could point out the way back to the road. Coming up beside him, she said, "Excuse me, but have you seen a horse wandering in the woods?"

Not looking up from his work, he shook his head and said softly, almost inaudibly, "No."

Mary said, "I guess that would have been hoping for too much good luck. Can you tell me in which direction I should go to reach the road?"

The hunter didn't utter a word. He just raised one blood-caked hand and pointed.

Mary looked in the direction he pointed and saw a tangle of trees and brush. She said, "Thank you. Do you know how far away the road is?"

Again, not looking up, he said softly, "Not far."

Mary started walking in the direction he indicated. As she walked, she wondered about the hunter. She had known many downcast people in her life, but he was different. He seemed less beaten down and more let down. As if life hadn't crushed his spirit, but instead, he had walked away from society.

Suddenly, she stopped. Where is the road? Was she still walking in the correct direction? As she stood there, she heard the unmistakable sound of a horse-drawn wagon. It was close, straight ahead. She headed towards it and soon found herself standing beside the road. She could just hear the wagon retreating to the south in the direction she would go if she were to continue her journey to Rennes-le-Chateau. But now, without a horse, it seemed very unlikely she could make it on her own. While she stood there, lost in indecision, she heard approaching hoofbeats. She looked north in the direction of the noise. For a moment, she hoped against hope that it was her horse returning. But instead, she saw seven or eight of the King's guards approaching her at a trot. Before she knew what she was doing, she had turned and plunged back into the woods in a panic. She didn't understand why she had run; surely they were no longer looking for her, if they had ever been. She supposed she fled merely out of habit.

One of the King's guards must have seen her, for he called out, "Halt, in the name of the king!" He then turned off the road and crashed through the thick underbrush. Mary found a thicket of brambles and dove headfirst into the concealment they offered, ignoring the thorns. Peering through the undergrowth, she could make out one of the King's guards walking his horse slowly through the woods. As he approached her concealed position, she heard a voice back at the road call out, "Gareth, leave the wench alone. We need to get to Avignon as soon as possible and don't have time for chasing every peasant that runs from you."

"Be quiet. This won't take long. The bird has gone to ground, but I can smell her fear." Then, in a quieter voice meant only for Mary's ears, he said, "Here, birdie, birdie, why do you run?"

Mary was about to break from cover as the man's horse drew closer when she heard a "twang" followed closely by a "thwack" as an arrow struck a tree right beside the King's man. The shaft of the arrow was directly in front of his face and only missed his head by inches. Mary saw him stop his horse and calmly study the shaft. Then, he looked off in the direction the arrow had come from and called out, "I believe you missed my head on purpose, archer, and since this environment is more suited to your fighting style than mine, I'll withdraw. Injuring my horse isn't worth the little birdie anyway. But should I catch you on the road…" and, leaving the consequences of the archer being caught on the road unsaid, he turned his horse around and left the woods.

Mary watched him disappear and then heard the voice of his companions laugh as they rode off. She was still afraid to move for some time after the hoofbeats had faded to nothing, concerned it might be a trick. But then she heard a voice say, "I believe you can come out now; they have truly gone."

Chapter 16

The next day, as William, Bertrand, and Louis made their way westward, William pondered his command, which now only consisted of three, including himself. He felt entirely at a loss for what to do. William questioned his ability to complete the mission, which he was beginning to think may no longer be relevant, given the revelations of the last few days. Although William told Louis it was none of his business, he couldn't stop thinking about what he had said and how he had spoken to Sergeant Bertrand. Shame overcame his pride, and he rode up to Bertrand. Clearing his voice, he said, "Sergeant Bertrand, I need to apologize to you. I had no right to speak to you as I did. It's just that I feel as though I've been asked to carry out a job that has grown beyond my abilities and even beyond my comprehension. I don't know what is happening to our Order, and I'm no longer certain I should continue to Rennes-le-Chateau."

"I accept your apology. At the risk of provoking your anger again, I would remind you that you were ordered to carry out a mission. Until someone countermands that order, you need to carry it out to the best of your ability and not worry about the things you cannot control," replied Bertrand without looking away from the road ahead.

"Thank you. Both for accepting my apology and for reminding me of my responsibility."

They rode on in silence. Louis was too far behind them for either to make out the words of his constant droning. The road they were on never seemed to open up, so the two men riding side-by-side had to raise a hand regularly to move a branch. William finally said, "This road doesn't seem well traveled. Do you know exactly where it leads?"

"I'm not certain. I believe it leads through Clermont and then on to Brive. From there, we can head south to Rennes-le-Chateau." After briefly pausing, Bertrand added, "Maybe I should tell you something. Before we left on this adventure, Grand Master Jacques de Molay told me a little about what was happening and how our mission fit into the situation. As Thomas the priest indicated, it seems there have been rumors that King Philip and his advisor and lawyer, Guillaume de Nogaret, have been planning something against us Templars. The Grand Master was not specific about what they were planning, either because he didn't know or because he didn't feel it was necessary to share that with me. Yet, I did not get the impression it was anything like what Father Thomas has claimed. I assumed it would be more along the lines of petitioning to the Pope that the Order should be forced to pay taxes on our lands or move more of our number out of France. From what the Grand Master told me, I had no idea they would attempt to arrest any of us. He also told me that no matter what happened, we and what we carry would be safe in Rennes-le-Chateau. He confided to me that although you were young and untested, he had great confidence in you."

William let that sink in for a moment. It made him feel both proud and unworthy to have the Grand Master trust him. Realizing he needed to respond to what he had just been told, William said, "Do you have any idea why the Grand Master would believe we would be safe in Rennes-le-Chateau?"

Bertrand answered, "We have always had a lot of support from that part of France. I know a lot of men from the craft guilds have been sent there to do work for the Order. Therefore, I assume we have defendable facilities there, although I've never been myself. I have no real knowledge about what we can expect when we arrive."

William was about to ask more about the type of support Sergeant Bertrand thought they could expect when they arrived at Rennes-le-Chateau, but he was interrupted by Louis' shrill whistle. It conveyed a sense of urgency, causing both men to stop their horses and turn in their saddles to look at Louis. Once Louis had their attention, he pointed behind him and said just loud enough for them to hear, "Riders approaching at a trot."

Bertrand looked at William and said, "Maybe one of us should get off the road so we could use the element of surprise if the situation calls for it."

William said, "That seems wise. You go. I'll stay on the road with Louis."

Bertrand, who could tell they didn't have much more time before the riders came into view, said, "Sir, no offense, but I've had a bit more experience lying than you. I believe I would be the better choice to parley with whoever approaches."

Knowing he was right and there was no time to argue, William nodded and rode his horse some twenty feet into the woods, turning to peer through the thick foliage.

As soon as William left the road, Bertrand turned his horse around and moved sideways to obscure the tracks of William's horse. Then he told Louis, "Get off the wagon and check the mules' hooves as if one had picked up a stone. If we go to fighting, you get under the wagon and stay out of the way."

Louis was about to argue that he was also a trained soldier and that he could help if it came to a fight. For that matter, he thought, he'd be the best choice to talk with whoever was approaching. Louis was sure he was a better storyteller than either William or the Sergeant. He'd never call it "lying," just spinning a good tale, but he could hear the horses drawing closer and knew there was no time to argue. He had just lifted the front hoof of one of the mules when the riders came into sight behind them.

Chapter 17

The men with clubs were there to keep the prisoners back. However, this was probably not needed as it appeared all the captives in the cell were sufficiently cowed and would cause no trouble. Henry grew increasingly angered as he saw many of his fellow knights quietly moan or cringe away from the center of the cell containing the evil men and their malevolent devices of persuasion. The four clergy members appeared to be in prayer while the servants set up the tools of their trade. Henry de Creon had never seen anyone tortured, nor had he ever seen a torture instrument before, but his imagination did allow him to guess at the uses of the devices.

After a moment, the clergy ended their prayer, and one of them spoke, "You men have been arrested and charged with heinous crimes against God and the Holy Church. You have been beguiled by the Devil and given yourselves over to the lusts of the flesh. We, brothers of the Holy Inquisition, are here to aid you in your road to redemption. My name is Father Raymon. I am the chief inquisitor, and I take this holy calling very seriously."

The prisoners in the cell were all moving away from the torturers and their tools of "redemption," except the few who would not give them the pleasure of thinking they were unsettled by the torturers in the least. Henry stood with those who refused to move away. One of the clergy members pointed a finger at one of the men, showing his lack of fear and defiance of the Inquisitionists by not shrinking away. Two of the guards went forward to escort the man to one of two solid wooden chairs sitting next to the tools of torture. The man neither blanched nor fought back but willingly stepped forward without the slightest hesitation as he took his seat, staring at the chief inquisitor with a look of disdain on his face. He was strapped to the chair, and a harness was buckled tightly around his forehead. This forehead harness had a strap that came off the front and was pulled over the top of the man's head and back down, allowing it to be buckled to the back of the chair. This had the effect of drawing his head back so that he was looking nearly straight up.

One of the clergy members took a seat at a small table and retrieved a tablet, ink, and a quill. Father Raymon said, "What is your name?"

The man replied in a clear voice, "I am Sir Garrard de La Longuedoc, Knight of the Temple, and as such, I am answerable only to the leaders of my Order and to the Holy Father himself. You have no right to treat me or any of my brothers in this manner."

This brief outburst caused Henry's heart to swell with pride. He had never met or heard of Sir Garrard before, but he felt pride in having the Order represented by this man. The short speech must have had a similar effect on many of the other men in the room, as there were grunts of agreement. Many of the men inched a little away from their positions along the walls. This caused the guards to take a more protective stance and look around at the men who outnumbered them many times over. For the first time, it seemed they appreciated that these men surrounding them were not just rabble, but men trained in the art of war.

The chief inquisitor acted as if he noticed none of this and said to the brother keeping the records of the proceedings, "Write that the prisoner's name is Garrard." After a brief pause, he continued, "Now, Garrard, when you were initiated into this heretical Order, tell me about how they had you deny Christ. Did they make you spit on the cross?"

This caused many of the men to grumble angrily, but with Garrard, it brought on a torrent of fury. He bellowed, "If you were not a priest and I was not strapped to this chair, I would have an apology from you for saying such a thing. Our initiations are secret, and I cannot reveal what we do, but I can tell you what we don't do. We do not deny Christ! We do not spit on the cross. If we were asked to deny Christ in order to join the Templars, why would over eighty of our brethren choose to be flayed alive or beheaded rather than deny Christ at the fall of Castle Safed?"

Again, the chief inquisitor said in a mild voice to the record keeper, "Garrard denies charges the first time he is asked." He then pointed to an instrument on the table, which one of the other inquisitors picked up. It was a pair of long-nosed pliers. While one of the guards held Garrard's mouth open, the inquisitor with the pliers slid a small wooden block into Garrard's mouth. He wedged it between Garrard's upper and lower teeth, forcing the mouth open wider than Henry thought possible while keeping the jaw attached. He then took the pliers, reached into the mouth, and with a twist, yanked out one of Garrard's teeth. The tooth was placed in a small

81

bag. This caused only a tiny spasm from Garrard in acknowledgment of the pain. But it caused the men who had previously seemed to find their backbones by Garrard's earlier words to begin to inch back toward the presumed protection of the walls.

Father Raymon asked in an almost bored voice, "Now, Garrard, do you admit to denying Christ?"

Garrard tried to speak, but the wooden block in his mouth made it impossible to understand his words. Father Raymon said, "Just shake your head yes or no. We have no need of speeches."

Garrard violently shook his head, "No."

Raymon pointed to a long, almost wire-thin device on the table. The plier-wielding priest took the new instrument and began to use the wire to probe in the empty socket where he had just extracted the tooth. Garrard again did not cry out, but he periodically spasmed as exposed nerves were pricked by the wire. After a minute or two of this probing, Father Raymond repeated his question and received the same negative response from Garrard. This resulted in another tooth being pulled and placed in the bag, and further probing in the newly empty socket. This continued for some time. Henry lost count of how many teeth were removed, but he knew there couldn't be many remaining. Garrard seemed to be near total exhaustion from the pain. Henry was surprised Garrard had not passed out during the questioning.

Father Raymon must have realized that Garrard was probably no longer feeling the full effect of the torture, so he told the record keeper that they were going to pause the questioning of Garrard and move on to another prisoner. To the room of prisoners, Father Raymon said, "Garrard is still refusing the mercy that the Mother Church is offering his soul. We will pause in our questioning of him and start with another. Guards, go get me one of the men lurking along the wall."

The guards advanced as men scattered to get out of their way. They captured a man who seemed too fearful to move and dragged him forward. As they began to strap him to the chair, he began to babble. At first, his words could not be understood, but Henry soon understood him: he was repeatedly saying, "I confess. I confess. I confess."

Father Raymon put a hand on the man's shoulder and said,

"All in due time, my son. We must follow the procedure so there is no misunderstanding."

Henry initially felt anger at the man's weakness, but then this turned to pity and finally to a blinding fury aimed at Father Raymon. Henry took two steps forward and said, "That is enough, you cowardly son of a whore. Is this how you get pleasure, torturing bound men? Pick up a sword and face me as a man, you worthless piece of horse shit." Then, everything went black.

Chapter 18

Mary never heard the hunter approach, yet he was standing right next to the thicket where she was hiding. She made her way out as carefully as possible, now aware of every thorn as she tried to extricate herself. Mary could now tell he was a young man not much older than herself; he stood, not looking at her but apparently waiting for her. She approached to within a few feet of where he stood and noticed that he visibly tensed as she drew near, as if fearful she might touch him.

"Thank you," she said in a quiet voice. "I don't know..." and then she burst into tears. All the exhaustion, fear, and frustration caught up to her all at once. After several minutes, she began to regain control of herself, and the crying turned to broken sobs and sniffles. Finally, she stopped. The entire time she cried, the young man never moved or said a word. As far as she could tell, he never even looked at her. She noticed that he stood so that the burned side of his face was away from her, either on purpose or by chance; she could not tell.

She said, "I'm sorry. I just don't know what to do. I'm tired and lost. My horse has run off." She felt herself begin to lose control again and stopped speaking.

With a brief sidelong glance, the young man said, "Follow me." And began to move away from her.

Mary stood there for a moment, not sure what to do. Should she follow? She knew nothing about this man. Was he safe? Was he sane? But her exhaustion, coupled with the helplessness she felt, left her with no real choice, so she followed him.

The young man returned to the deer he had killed earlier and draped it across his shoulders. As he did this, Mary asked, "What is your name?"

Again, without looking at her, he said quietly, "Darrick." They began to move deeper into the woods. Mary had to walk quickly to keep up with Darrick, for although he seemed to be moving with little effort, he swiftly made his way through the jumble of brush and branches that tried to trip her up at every step. After perhaps thirty minutes, she began to tire of the pace and the silence. She said, "I'm Mary, by the way, in case you're wondering." Darrick may or may not have heard. She could not tell. So, she tried again and said, "Where are we going, and how much further is it?"

Darrick said softly, "Just ahead."

After another five or ten minutes, they came to a small clearing. There were the remnants of a campfire with a six-foot log lying beside it that apparently acted as a bench. There was a roughly constructed table off a little distance from the campfire. Mary saw nothing that resembled a house or dwelling of any type. She was just beginning to think this must be Darrick's hunting camp and that he lived elsewhere, but then he seemed to disappear into a thicket. As Mary approached the thicket, she noticed a cleverly designed opening that made it difficult, if not impossible, to see unless you knew where to look. Mary tentatively entered the opening and found a slowly curving pathway through the branches and vines. It was dark in the tunnel. She almost called out to Darrick when her eyes adjusted enough to see the open entrance ahead that showed the red flicker of a small fire beyond. The doorway seemed to be mounted directly into the side of a mound of dirt. She entered the room just as Darrick kindled the embers of the firepit into a small flame, changing the glow it gave off from a bloody red to a more cheerful orangish-yellow.

Darrick's home was one room with a pit fireplace in the center. There was no chimney, just an opening in the ceiling directly above the firepit that allowed the smoke to escape. There was another roughly made table that appeared to be used for a variety of tasks along one wall and a pile of animal skins used for a bed along another. Above the firepit, a kettle hanging from a tripod gave off the smell of stewed meat and vegetables. The aroma caused Mary's stomach to rumble; she realized she was very hungry.

Darrick lay the deer on the table and began to skin the carcass. When he heard Mary's stomach growl, he wiped his hands on a piece of cloth, retrieved a wooden bowl and spoon, and scooped some stew. Without a word, he handed the bowl to Mary. She ate ravenously. It wasn't the best stew: there was no seasoning. There was meat, potatoes, and some other unrecognizable root or tuber. She was thankful for it, all the same, as it was hot and filling.

After Darrick removed the hide from the deer, he deftly cut out the backstraps, cutting several chucks out of one and throwing them in the stewpot. Darrick then retrieved a few potatoes and a turnip from a niche cut directly into the dirt wall, diced them up, and added them to the stew pot along with water from a clay pitcher. Mary, her stomach full and feeling oddly safe around the strange, quiet man she had just met, suddenly felt very sleepy. Even though it was only late morning, Mary had not slept well the previous two nights, and the stress of the last couple of days overcame her. As there was no chair or stool in the room, she went to one of the dirt walls and sat down, almost instantly falling asleep.

Chapter 19

Henry woke lying on his back. At first, he was confused. He had been dreaming of being at his family home as a boy. The dream was of the time when he was thirteen or fourteen years old and had a terrible toothache. He hid it from everyone in his family because he feared they would pull it. Eventually, the pain grew so bad he could not eat or drink, and his father realized what was going on. He took young Henry out to the stables, found a pair of pliers the blacksmith used to shoe the horses, and told Henry to open his mouth. Although Henry was frightened, he knew better than to disobey his father. He stepped forward and dutifully opened his mouth wide. His father reached in with the pliers and yanked out the offending tooth.

Henry's eyes teared with the sudden blast of pain, but he did not cry out. His father patted him on the shoulder and said, "That's good, son. Don't ever cry out in pain. If others see a weakness in you, they will take advantage of it. Since you are my fifth son, I'll not have lands to give you, but I will ensure you are trained well enough to go out and seize your own lands. Although I can only strengthen your arm and help train your mind, you must learn to strengthen your will. You must resolve what you will do in your heart and never show weakness or fear. Now go inside and ask your mother for a clove to suck on; it'll reduce the pain and make your breath not smell like a sheep took a crap in your mouth."

Henry heard the soft whinny of a horse as he turned to go. It sounded funny, not quite like a horse, more like a child softly sobbing. He was suddenly fully awake and recalled what had happened before the world had gone dark. One of the guards must have struck him with a bludgeon. The sound was not a horse or a child but one of his fellow Templars. The man was crying and confessing to everything Father Raymon asked him about and was even making up things on his own to confess to. The record keeper seemed to be having trouble keeping up with the torrent of confessions coming out of the man because Father Raymon kept asking him to slow down.

Henry was not lying on the floor as he first supposed. He was strapped to a bedlike frame made entirely of metal. He assumed the man who was confessing was the second Templar who had been brought forward. Henry could see that Garrard was still strapped to his chair, temporarily being ignored by his tormentors.

As Henry looked around, Father Raymon noticed him and said, "Ah, you are awake. I think it is time we listen to another confession. Guard, please move the brazier up so that we may begin to cleanse this man's soul. Now, what is your name?"

Henry said, "Henry de Creon, Knight of the Temple."

Henry's feet were bare and dangling over the end of the "bed" he was tied to. As he heard the guard slide the brazier under his feet, he felt the sudden heat and smelled the sickly-sweet smell of burning flesh.

Raymon leaned over him and said, "Did you deny Christ upon your initiation into this dark brotherhood? Would you like to confess now or later after your feet become useless?"

Henry did not trust himself to vocalize a response to this question. He was afraid that if he opened his mouth, only screams would come out. His feet felt like they were on fire, so he shook his head. After what seemed like an eternity but was probably less than a minute, Raymon had them slide the brazier back. His feet still hurt like a thousand pinpricks of pain, but there was a sudden decrease in intensity. Again, Father Raymon's face appeared over his, "Are you ready to confess now? Did you deny Christ during your initiation into the Templars?"

Finding his tongue, Henry said through clenched teeth, "No."

Father Raymon mildly nodded, looking down toward Henry's feet, and said, "He needs more incentive to tell the truth."

Suddenly, the searing pain returned. This process of cooking Henry's feet and questioning him continued for some time, but Henry refused to confess to anything. At one point, Raymon told him that he could just admit to spitting on the cross. Telling Henry that the cross was the evil instrument used to kill Christ, and there was no harm in acknowledging that. But Henry would not confess to anything he had not done. Additionally, Henry was concerned that if he started to admit to anything, he would keep on confessing to everything they accused him of, like the other poor Templar.

Henry passed out from the pain several times. When this happened, they would slide the brazier away and wait for him to regain consciousness. Henry had no idea how long he was questioned. It all ran together in his tormented mind. He worried that he would be crippled for life. He envisioned himself with blackened stubs at the end of his legs, begging for alms at a city gate. The pain grew so great that even when he was conscious, he was aware of little more than the pain. He no longer heard the questions and, therefore, could not respond. His mind screamed to stop the pain, but he had succumbed to a temporary madness and was no longer cognizant of anything except the unending agony. Raymon finally said, "I think we have done enough for the Kingdom of God today."

Henry was unbound from his "bed." He and Garrard were removed from the large common room that housed all the other prisoners and taken to one of the small cells used by visiting monks. They were locked in a room together, with a guard stationed at the door. Garrard cared for Henry's feet as best he could. Although the burns were horribly painful, Garrard was certain Henry would recover fully. Although the feet were blackened and blistered along the entirety of his soles, the torturers had expertly backed the brazier away so that the heat did not burn so deeply that it deadened his sense of pain along the bottoms of his feet. Garrard told Henry he had seen men in Outremer fully recover from much worse burns.

Chapter 20

Sir William sat astride his horse just far enough off the road that he would not easily be seen but could still see out through the branches. As he strained to hear the approaching riders on the road, he smelled a noxious odor. He looked around to find the source and discovered, off to his left, the remains of a stag. It was lying crushed beneath a large tree branch. William contemplated the image before him and wondered how this could have happened. Was the deer standing under the widow maker when it chanced to fall? Perhaps he had been sleeping, and the branch gave way from its parent tree and struck the hapless deer. He wondered about the crazy misfortune that would surround such an event. Suddenly, his reverie was broken by the sounds of the approaching riders.

Three riders rode up behind the wagon. The first rider shouted in a gruff voice, "Move this piece of shit off the road."

Louis, who had just lifted the leg of one of the mules so that he appeared to be examining the hoof, said, "Yes. Sir. My apologies for hogging this path that passes for a road in these parts." Louis lowered the mule's leg and took hold of one of the leads. He began to direct the mules and wagon off to the side of the road.

The man with the gruff voice rode around the wagon's edge. He was about to deliver a blow to William with his foot when he noticed Sergeant Bertrand riding slowly toward him from just up the road. Sergeant Bertrand rode to within a few feet, stopped his destrier, and said, "I'm sorry that we have inconvenienced you, good sirs, but the lad was checking the mule's hoof. It seems the beast was limping; must have picked up a stone."

By this time, the other two riders had moved around the wagon. All three were in boiled leather armor with bits of chain mail protecting the joints. They carried themselves as men who knew how to defend themselves. Yet, they displayed no devices indicating they were bound to a lord and, therefore, were most likely free riders. Bertrand took all this in at a glance, knowing that unattached soldiers like these were no better than a higher class of highwaymen. Yet, they likely would have had some formal training with weapons and could prove very dangerous. Without any conscious thought, Bertrand began to formulate a plan of attack just in case the need arose.

The gravelly-voiced man said, "What have we here? You're wearing fine armor and sitting on a nice-looking war horse. What might you be protecting in the wagon?"

Bertrand looked at the wagon and said in a friendly tone, "Books. A lord in Macon hired me to protect his library, which he was moving to a country home he has near Brive."

The gravelly-voiced man said with a snort, "Books? Who needs protection for books? I think you're lying to me, sir."

Bertrand's gaze slowly shifted back to the man. He said in a tone that was no longer friendly, "I'm no sir, and I believe you had better move along before you offend me any further." Then, he wound the reins around his left fist once, sat up straighter in the saddle, and moved his right hand to the hilt of his sword.

The gravelly-voiced man looked at first as if he might just move down the road, as Bertrand suggested, but then an evil grin slowly spread across his face. He said, "You have the look of an experienced soldier, and if you were a few years younger, I'd have likely taken your advice and begged your pardon to boot. But you're getting a bit long in the tooth. I think your bark is worse than your bite, old man. Boys, check the wagon and see what we have here," as he said this, he reached for his sword.

Before the two other men could move or the gravelly-voiced man could fully retrieve his sword from its scabbard, Sergeant Bertrand kicked spurs to his horse's flanks and drew his sword in one fluid movement, charging the three men. William was as surprised as the free riders and was still trying to get his horse out of the woods when Bertrand collided with the gravelly-voiced man. Bertrand's sword swung wide as the gravelly-voiced man wheeled his horse to the right. Bertrand continued his charge toward the other two riders. The first, he slashed across the throat and must have hit an artery since blood flew out in a spray for several feet, and the man toppled from his horse, grasping his neck as he died.

The second man held a bastard sword in a two-handed grip. He appeared quite content to let Bertrand charge him and was prepared to parry Bertrand's swing. It was a mistake that cost him his life since Bertrand failed to swing his sword but instead leaned forward and held the sword out straight. He drove the point into the man's chest with the full weight of his body and his charging horse. The impact sent a savage jarring up Bertrand's arm. He knew better

91

than to try to extract the sword or to attempt to maintain possession of it as he had driven it all the way through the man up to the quillon. He quickly released his grip on the sword's hilt as he came abreast of the dying man. The man with Bertrand's sword protruding from his chest maintained his seat. His muscles continued to move even as his brain struggled to comprehend that it was shutting down. The dying man's training continued to respond to the fight; he brought his own sword across his body in an arch that ended at his side as Bertrand rode past.

Bertrand felt a sharp pain across his back as he continued past the man. He reined in his charging horse and began to wheel him about. Bertrand reached down to his saddle and gripped the handle of the warhammer. As he and his horse came around, he let the momentum of his mount's turn bring the hammer up and out in an arc that ended with the spike side of the hammerhead coming to rest in the temple of the gravelly-voiced man's head as he had spurred his horse and was attempting to attack Bertrand from behind.

It was over before William could offer any assistance in fighting the men. He didn't think the free riders were even aware of his presence. All three men lay dead, and Bertrand was looking at William with what William took to be a look of contempt at his lack of action. That is, until Bertrand fell sideways out of his saddle. William quickly dismounted and rushed to Bertrand, who lay in a heap beside his horse.

Louis crawled from beneath the wagon and joined William at Bertrand's side. They could see no wounds, and William thought that perhaps Bertrand had taken a blow to the head that stunned him. But then Bertrand said, "One of those bastards struck my back as I rode past him."

William and Louis rolled Bertrand onto his side. There was a gash that cut through the light leather armor on the back and opened the flesh from just below his neck all the way to his waist. There was a lot of blood, and they could see the bone and muscle and what could only be his organs.

William told Louis, "Get some water and something clean we can use for a bandage from the wagon while I get this armor off him. We also need something to pack in this gash and some way to hold it closed so that we can stop the bleeding."

By the time they had slowed the bleeding, bandaged the wound as best they could, and laid him out in the wagon, Bertrand was very white from loss of blood and shivering as if he were freezing.

William said, "We need a place to hold up for a few days so the Sergeant can heal. You keep moving down the road with the Sergeant in the back of the wagon, and I'll ride ahead to see what I can find. I will return as soon as I locate a usable location. If I haven't returned by nightfall, pull off the road and make camp for the night. Do not light a fire tonight. Continue down the road as soon as it is light enough to see where you are going. If I haven't found anything by midmorning tomorrow, I'll turn around and meet you before nightfall tomorrow evening."

Louis, with a look at the resting Bertrand, said, "What about him? What do I do? I have no skill at healing."

William said, "Just keep him comfortable, give him water, and change the bandages if you can find something clean to replace the old ones. As long as we can keep the bleeding slowed down, he has a chance."

William road hard the rest of the day and on into the night. He knew he should stop as it was not only nighttime but extra dark due to the thick forest. Yet William felt he owed it to the Sergeant to find help.

After he suddenly woke, almost falling out of the saddle, William realized he must stop for the night, or he would soon be walking, and his horse would be lame. The next morning, William approached a town of some size and discovered it was Clermont. He thought maybe it was a good sign, that perhaps God was guiding him to this town because Clermont was the starting point of the First Crusade. It was here that Pope Urban II preached the crusade to free Jerusalem in 1095. And that crusade led to the establishment of the Knights Templar.

1118

Sir Hugh De Paynes, a knight of the lower nobility who had fought to reclaim Jerusalem, went before King Baldwin II, the Christian King of Jerusalem. Hugh de Paynes wanted to form an order of knights dedicated to protecting pilgrims traveling to the Holy Land. But what truly made this Order unique was that they

93

wished to take monastic vows. They wanted to take holy vows of perpetual poverty, chastity, and obedience.

Hugh de Paynes and eight other knights claimed that their order would protect the pilgrims who were now flocking to Jerusalem to visit the holy sites, believing that since the Christian armies had taken the Holy Land from the infidels, they were safe to travel to Outremer. Yet nothing could be further from the truth. There were roving bands of Muslims and Christians willing to rob, murder, rape, or force into slavery any pilgrim foolish enough to travel in small numbers. But even worse, the very land itself was inhospitable. The average European had no idea what a desert actually was.

King Baldwin II offered Hugh De Paynes and the other eight knights a portion of the al-Aqsa Mosque, which had been built over the original Temple of Solomon. It was from this location that this new order of knights took their name and would forever be known as Pauperes commilitones Christi Templique Salomonis (the Poor Fellow-Soldiers of Christ and the Temple of Solomon).

For the next several years, there is little record of the activity of these nine knights and their attendants. Some have claimed that they spent the first nine years digging on the Temple grounds, searching for something they believed was buried there. Others think they were about the business of protecting the pilgrims, as they stated. Whatever their activities were, the King must have been pleased with them, for in 1127, King Baldwin II wrote a letter to Bernard of Clairvaux (later Saint Bernard), one of the most respected men in Christendom at the time. The letter asked Bernard to contact the Pope, Honorius II (a former pupil of Bernard). He wanted Bernard to request that the Papacy officially recognize the Order and aid them in establishing a Rule to govern the life of the Knights Templar. Bernard was a cousin of Hugh De Payne and the nephew of another of the original nine knights. He enthusiastically contacted the Pope to pave the way for this new order of monk-knights.

Hugh de Paynes was even then on his way to seek an audience with the Pope regarding the formal recognition of the warrior monks. When he and his companions arrived at the Papal court, they found the Pope very welcoming. Everything the knights had hoped for and more was lavished upon them. With Bernard and *the Pope's support, land and money were soon donated to aid the Templars, and men began joining throughout Europe. The Order would teach the men the new Rule that Bernard had written himself and train knights to fight together, something that was new to European medieval military groups. Suddenly, the Poor Fellow-Soldiers of Christ and the Temple of Solomon were on the road to becoming one of Christendom's most powerful and wealthy armies. Less than 200 years later, the Monarch of France would notice and make plans to acquire that wealth and crush their power.*

As William entered the town of Clermont, he found a tavern on the east side of town and inquired about someone who could help with an injured man. An elderly man named Michael, who worked at the pub, said he had some training as a barber-surgeon and would help for a price. William gave the man enough coins to make it worth his while to accompany him back up the road. Michael grabbed a few supplies, saddled a horse, and followed William out of town at a steady trot.

It was late afternoon before they ran into Louis, Sergeant Bertrand, and the wagon. The barber/surgeon, Michael, removed the bandages and made some grumbling sounds about young idiots. The Sergeant stayed quiet while Michael probed and pushed on the wound. Finally, Michael said, "You're lucky you got your man to me when you did. There are already signs of putrefaction. You might have cleaned the wound before you wrapped it in filthy rags. I'm going to have to burn away the rotting flesh and try to sew the wound closed. It's going to hurt like hell."

Bertrand finally spoke, saying, "Get on with it and quit complaining. You're not the one who gets a hot poker in his back."

Michael laughed and said, "I can see by your scars that this is not the first time you've been used as a pincushion, so I won't try to frighten you with warnings about how much it will hurt. But I will offer you a bit of drink to help with the pain."

"That I'll gladly accept," Bertrand replied.

About an hour later, Sergeant Bertrand was lying, seemingly unconscious, in the wagon, and Michael was wiping the blood off his instruments. William approached the barber-surgeon and asked, "Will he be all right?"

Michael replied, with a glance toward the Sergeant, "I don't know, he lost a lot of blood. He made it this long, though, so he should be fine as far as that goes. There's just no way to know. If you can stay in Clermont for a few days, I will keep an eye on him. It all depends on how things go for the next couple of days. I have mercuric chloride, which I acquired in the Holy Lands from an Islamic healer who had no further need of it. I can apply it to the wound, which may help. If there are more signs of corruption, it will have to be dealt with aggressively, and that, or the loss of blood, may still kill him. There's no way to know."

Michael mounted his horse. Before he rode off, he looked down at William and, in a lowered voice, said, "I don't like the look of that wound. He's tough and has probably had worse injuries, but he's getting on in years. Older men die from injuries that don't even slow a younger man. Get to Clermont and come straight to the bar where you found me." With that, he rode back to town.

William looked at Louis and said, "Get things packed up. We have a couple of hours of daylight, and I want to get as far as possible before we stop for the night."

Chapter 21

Darrick noticed Mary had fallen asleep, so he retrieved a bear skin, laid it over her, and returned to butchering the deer.

Darrick knew he should talk to the girl, but he didn't know how. He had lived alone most of his life and seldom spoke to anyone anymore. Darrick stayed well away from where others lived. He hunted for food and made his clothes from skins. He would sell pelts and meat to buy the few supplies he needed. Although Darrick was born free and should have had the opportunity to live a more conventional life, at the age of six, he lost everything in a fire.

1288 AD

It was a dreadfully cold November night. The wind was howling outside, blowing the snow, which was usually not very heavy, into drifts three to four feet high. Darrick would never forget that night. His mother and father were sitting around the fireplace, huddled together in the enormous skin of the bear his father had killed several years before. The bear had been one of the great brown ones from the South. His father was off hunting alone when he came upon the bear: he emptied his quiver of arrows, yet the bear kept coming. Just as Darrick's father was about to pull his knife, knowing running would be a foolish and deadly act, the bear fell and died at his feet. The skin was warm, and his parents often slept together in it on cold winter nights.

Darrick was sitting not far from them, oiling his father's bow and fixing arrows, a chore he had just recently been taught to do by his father. His infant sister, Bernadette, was asleep beside their parents on another animal-skin rug. The house, though small, was warm and cozy. Due to the bad weather and the deer his father had killed that day, the home was even more comfortable.

Darrick held up one of his father's arrows, identified by the wide silver ring before the feathers. He ensured he had glued all the feathers on straight when he heard his mother cry out. As Darrick looked up, he saw that the bear skin rug his parents were wrapped in somehow had caught on fire from the blaze in the fireplace. At first, he didn't realize the seriousness of the situation. It began so small, and it seemed to happen so gradually. But before he had even moved from his seat, the skin erupted into flames.

His mother was in a panic to free herself and was trying to rescue Bernadette from the flames that were quickly spreading. His father was trying to remove the blazing skin but was confounded by his wife's efforts. For a moment, Darrick couldn't move. His eyes were transfixed on the horrible scene before him. He saw his father become a human torch. He held his wife in one of his great arms and, in the other, Bernadette. They were all ablaze along with that side of the house. His father took two steps toward the front door and then fell.

Darrick watched with fear as the bodies of his mother, father, and sister seemed to melt into one. It was the flames themselves that woke Darrick from his disbelief and drove him from his house. He stumbled outside and ran about a hundred feet before he sat down in the deep snow. He sat and watched as his life burned away. Soon, the snow started melting all around the inferno. The reflection of the flames dancing in the water caused Darrick to become hypnotized.

He remembered nothing after that until early the next morning when a woodsman, who was coming to see Darrick's father about a trade, found Darrick sitting in front of the smoldering embers of his life, half frozen in the snow.

As Darrick came to, he noticed two things. One, he had been burned in the fire: his face, hands, and part of his arms had been permanently scarred in the inferno. And two, he was still holding the arrow he had been fixing; it was all Darrick had left, the only inheritance he would ever receive. The woodsman took Darrick back to his house, warmed him up, put some salve on the burns, and put him to bed.

Following the death of his family, Darrick stayed with the woodcutter's family until he was thirteen. He didn't talk much, and although he did the chores he was assigned and ate with the family, he never became a part, in any real way, of the woodcutter's family.

At the age of thirteen, Darrick decided to move away and start his own life. Even at such a young age, Darrick had become quite a tracker, and his arrows were always true. Darrick moved approximately 100 miles away, which was a considerable distance for people to travel at that time. Many people never traveled more than thirty miles from the place where they were born during their entire lives. Darrick moved into the woods near Paris but far enough away to avoid people. At the time, Darrick took up residence in the woods south of Paris, which was well known for being peaceful. Not because the people in it were all honest, hard workers, but rather because the seneschal of the town ruled with an iron fist and had many men to enforce his law. The seneschal's name was Rass. Rass wanted peace not for the good of the people but for the sake of his purse. Rass was a very wise businessman and knew that peace, especially peace enforced by his men, was good for business.

Darrick didn't move near Paris because he liked the town itself, but because it was a large town with a forest nearby filled with a variety of game. Thus, he had a better chance of selling the game he hunted. Darrick only ventured into the town proper when he had to sell his wares.

It was by mere chance or maybe fate (if you believe in such a thing) that Darrick happened to be going to Paris one hot afternoon. He was making a trip into town to sell some pelts and smoked meat. In the eight years he had lived near Paris, Darrick's smoked meat had become a favorite item among some of the people. While still outside the town gates, Darrick saw a detachment of the seneschal's men on horseback. It was common practice to step off the road and bow your head as the seneschal's men passed.

To start with, Darrick was not much for doing the "common practices," and he didn't feel much loyalty toward or fear of the seneschal or his men. To him, they were crooks and thugs. As the men approached Darrick, he continued to walk past them as if they weren't there. He also didn't move off the road, although he did move to the side, which gave them plenty of room.

As fortune would have it, Hailf, Rass's chief henchman, was leading the detachment. If it had been one of the other captains, he might have just yelled something at Darrick or maybe stopped and harassed him a bit. But Hailf was not a pleasant fellow to those who didn't respect him. Hailf wasn't really an evil man; he was just ambitious, and his views were a little distorted. Hailf's mother had died during childbirth, and his father, Stien, who raised him, was an unforgiving and, often, cruel man. He had instilled in Hailf the fear of authority and the honor of hard work. However, his methods were a bit extreme.

As Hailf reached Darrick, he stopped his line of men and

stared as Darrick walked past him with no show of recognition. Hailf motioned for some of his men to cut Darrick off. As Darrick approached the end of the line of men, he found himself face-to-face with three men. One of them lowered his spear and aimed the point at Darrick's chest. Darrick stopped in his tracks and looked at the man holding the spear. The spearman noticed Darrick's scarred face and said to his comrades, "God, look at this one! I've seen men with burns before, but his face is like something from a mummer's tale." The other men laughed, but Darrick acted as if he hadn't heard.

Hailf climbed down from his horse and made his way back to where Darrick stood. He placed one hand on the spear shaft and pushed it down as his other hand clapped Darrick on the shoulder. "What have we here?" Hailf said. "Possibly the flames have blinded him, and he didn't see us? Is that it? Are you blind, good sir?" he said to Darrick.

Darrick again said nothing, partly because he didn't really know what to say and partly because he was unused to physical contact, and Hailf's hand on his shoulder made him very uncomfortable.

Hailf looked closer at Darrick and said, "No, it appears you can see; perhaps you're just stupid or ignorant. I'm afraid we will need to instruct you." Hailf pushed Darrick to the ground and kicked him hard in the stomach.

Darrick's load of meat and pelts fell from his back, and one of the men grabbed them. Suddenly, Darrick was hauled from the dirt road and held by two men-at-arms while Hailf pummeled him repeatedly in the midsection and landed a few sharp blows to his face. Darrick was still conscious, although just barely, when Hailf, tired of the game, told one of his men, "Please continue the lesson until the pupil has been properly educated." Hailf remounted his horse and started up the road with all but the three soldiers who remained to make an example of Darrick and his lack of respect.

Mercifully, the first blow from the man who had taken over was hard and straight to the middle of Darrick's face, and he instantly passed out.

When he came to, he was naked, and his wrists were bound to a tree with his own bowstring. He couldn't see clearly as one of his eyes was completely swollen shut. The other was partly crusted over with dried blood. His back was to the road, but he could hear foot traffic and the occasional horse. No one stopped to help him, and he wasn't surprised; assisting an individual Hailf was making an example of was a good way to become an example yourself. As he looked around, he could make out his bow a couple of feet in front of him; it had been broken along with all his arrows. Darrick saw no sign of his clothes or his bundle of dried meat and skins that he was going to sell in the market. He didn't think he had any broken bones, but he couldn't stand up tied to the tree the way he was. Darrick didn't have the strength to try to undo his bonds, which were cutting so deeply into his wrists that his hands were numb. He sat there for some time, trying to work up the energy and courage to ask for help when he passed out again.

He was lying on his back when he came to the second time. His face was being washed, and the most beautiful woman he had ever seen was standing over him. She was saying, "This must be the work of that animal, Hailf. Oh, I think he's coming around. Can you hear me?"

Darrick tried to rise, but the man who had been wiping the blood from his face laid a restraining hand on his chest and said, "Not yet, lad, give it a minute."

The woman repeated, "Do you hear me?"

Darrick didn't speak, but he nodded his head, which hurt like hell. He then managed to sit up a little as the man kneeling beside him helped. Either the man or the woman had thrown a cloak over his nakedness, for which he was grateful.

The woman said, "Get him on my horse, John. We'll take him to the Hospitaller's commandery near the South gate."

Darrick recalled neither the ride to the city nor anything for the rest of that day. The following day, he awoke feeling very stiff and sore all over. He still couldn't see out of his left eye, and as he raised a hand to it, a voice as sweet as honey said, "No. Leave the bandage alone. They said the swelling should go down in a few days, and hopefully, the eye itself will be fine."

Darrick managed to say, "Who are you, and why would you risk helping me?"

The woman said, "My name is Francia, and I risked nothing. Hailf is an animal, but he would not dare bother me. My family is very highly placed, and the imbecile has been trying to get my hand

101

in marriage since I was twelve years old, as if that would ever happen. Now, if you think you can walk, we should probably leave. They said you have no broken bones other than your nose. The Hospitallers don't really like helping people who are not a part of their Order or who are not on a pilgrimage. They only agreed to help you because my father has donated a great deal of land to them."

Over the next few days, Darrick stayed with the servants of Lord Pajote, the father of Lady Francia. Lord Pajote was more inclined to send Derrick on his way, not liking the way his daughter had gotten herself involved in the business of the King's men. But Lady Francia had begged her father to allow Darrick to stay until he was at least well enough to walk back to his home in the woods. After much pleading, Lord Pajote relented and told his daughter, "As soon as he is capable of walking to his forest hovel, he is to be gone."

Lady Francia visited with him often. One day, she and Darrick went for a walk in the garden. Darrick spoke little, but Lady Francia seemed not to be put off by this, and Darrick began to feel comfortable, and oddly, he also felt ill at ease around her. On the last day, Lady Francia told Darrick that she was sad because he had healed so quickly, as it meant he would soon be leaving. Darrick dared to hope that Francia genuinely liked him. As they were walking, she slid an arm into his and kissed him on the cheek, not his good cheek but his burned and scarred one. He wasn't sure what to do or say, so he acted as if it didn't happen, yet it was all he could think about.

The next morning, Lord Pajote sent Lady Francia off to see a cousin in another part of the city before the sun was up. He also had the servants prepare a traveling meal for Darrick and gather his few possessions. Darrick met Lord Pajote in the main hall in the early morning. In a friendly tone, Lord Pajote said, "Darrick, I believe you have healed sufficiently to return to your home. My daughter has enjoyed your stay here, but she needs to get on with her responsibilities. I'm sure you have work that needs to be attended to. Perhaps someday, I will have the chance to try some of the smoked meat I hear you prepare so exquisitely. I have had the cooks prepare a meal you can eat on the road, as I'm sure you are anxious to return to your woods and your life."

Darrick was caught off guard and, again, being at a loss for words, replied, "Thank you, my Lord."

Lord Pajote said, "There's a good man." He turned and quickly left Darrick standing alone in the room. Darrick watched him go and stood there until a servant approached, handing him a bundle of his belongings and some food wrapped in cheesecloth.

As the servant escorted him to the front gates of the estate, Darrick asked, "Is Lady Francia about? I want to say goodbye."

In a clipped tone, the servant said, "Her Ladyship is not on the premises, nor is she likely to be here for the next few days." And with that, Darrick began his walk back to his dwelling in the woods.

When Darrick finally returned to the city, it was several months later. He had made a new bow and arrows and had done a good deal of hunting, so that he had plenty of smoked meat to sell. In addition, Darrick had tanned a bear pelt with great care, which he intended to give Francia as a thank-you. Darrick noticed he was oddly excited as he packed for the trip. While walking to the city in the predawn light, he imagined how Lady Francia would be overjoyed at the bear skin and maybe kiss him again, perhaps on the lips. He walked by the location where Hailf's men had tied him to the tree and thought, "Really wasn't a bad thing; if not for that incident, I never would have met Lady Francia."

When he approached the house of Lord Pajote, he began to feel some trepidation. He knocked at the servant's entrance door. A scullery maid answered the door and said, "We are in no need of meat," and started to close the door.

Darrick said, "Sorry, but I am here to see Lady Francia. Is she about?" The servant laughed, "Why would she see you? Be gone! And besides, she doesn't live here anymore. After marrying the seneschal's man, she lives near the castle on the hill."

"She married?" Darrick asked with disbelief.

The scullery maid said, "Of course, she married Captain Hailf. The marriage was arranged years ago." She closed the door without waiting for Darrick to interrupt her again with foolish questions.

Darrick stood there for a moment, uncertain what to do or think. Had everything been a game for her? He had no answers.

The incident only reinforced his belief that it was not worth developing a relationship with others. He decided that this was the

last time he would believe anyone and, from now on, he would stay
out of the city proper of Paris. The woods provided more than he
needed. When he had enough smoked meat and skins to sell or
trade, he would do all his business outside the city gates.

And now, here was some other woman. He looked over at her, sleeping under the bear skin he had originally prepared as a gift for another. He made up his mind then and there: as soon as she woke, he would take her to the outskirts of Paris, and she could find her way from there.

Chapter 22

Odo had been in the large common room, which was mostly used for meals. He had been there for almost a week now. During that time, he noticed only two guards were watching them during the day and only one at night. The guards paid little attention to their prisoners, who whispered amongst themselves and remained as unobtrusive as possible. There was only one door in and out of the common room, so the guards remained near the door and ensured no one left or entered without their permission.

The men and boys of the Templars around Odo did nothing but sit, whisper, shit, piss, and occasionally eat the small amount of food that was given to them. Odo could already feel he was growing weaker and more apathetic in the few days he had been there, and he knew it would only get worse as time went on. He determined that he would not let that happen; he was going to get out of there.

He decided nighttime would be his best opportunity. The doors never appeared to be locked, only guarded, and many of the overnight guards slept in the early morning hours. Odo thought he might be able to slip past the guard, and once out of the common hall, he could work his way to the stables in the dark of night. Once there, he could climb onto the roof and get over the outer wall. Louis had told Odo that he had "escaped" the Templar grounds that way at night on several occasions for a drink and a decent meal. Louis had tried to get Odo to join him once or twice, but although Odo liked Louis, he was not one to readily follow Louis in his schemes. Additionally, he enjoyed the strictly ordered life of a Templar and didn't feel the need to escape it, even temporarily.

That very night, the guard who showed up to watch them seemed to have been drinking before his arrival for guard duty, which wasn't uncommon. Late in the night, as he pretended to sleep, Odo noticed that the guard had smuggled a skin of something in with him and was periodically taking swigs. Shortly before dawn, the guard fell asleep. He had seated himself on the top step leading to the door out of the dining room. Odo had been waiting for this, but when the time for him to act had finally arrived, he felt that maybe it was too late. The sun would be up at any time, and his chance of a successful escape would decrease rapidly if he couldn't move in the shadows. Odo looked around. All the other men in the room appeared to be asleep also. He slowly rose and began to creep toward the door and the sleeping guard as quietly as possible. Odo was just a few feet in front of the door when one of his fellow prisoners started to talk in his sleep. This was not uncommon and seemed to be caused by all the stress they were under. Over time, they had all grown accustomed to it. Rarely did it cause anyone to wake unless the man started to yell or scream, which did occasionally happen.

Odo froze and stared at the guard, praying he would not wake up. It seemed long minutes had passed before the man finally quieted back to sleep, and Odo could continue toward the door. He cautiously covered the last few feet and reached a hand forward, applying just enough pressure to open the door slowly. However, nothing happened. Odo pushed a little harder, but still nothing happened. He tried one last time, hoping the door was just stuck, but fearing he was wrong about it being unlocked. Suddenly, Odo was struck on the back of the head and fell to one knee.

"You think you were just going to walk through a locked door? You lot truly are fools," the guard said, kicking Odo in the ribs.

Odo was stunned but conscious. He slumped to the ground and lay on his back, cursing his own stupidity. Of course, they would lock the door. The guard seemed to lose interest in him, and few of the men even woke. Those who did just ignored the altercation for fear it might spill over onto them. After a few minutes, Odo got unsteadily to his feet. He felt like his eyes were spinning around in his head. He felt somewhat unsure of everything around him, as if he were in a dream. Odo stumbled around until he finally found his way back to where he usually slept and lay down.

Chapter 23

Thomas, the priest, woke with a start. Someone was opening the door to his cell. His eyes had adjusted to the near-complete darkness to such an extent that when the door opened, and the light flooded in, he was blinded by the intense glare. As his eyes slowly became accustomed to the brightness, he could make out the shape of a man standing in the doorway. Thomas had reflexively slunk to the far wall away from the door as it had begun to open. The man in the doorway could not see Thomas in the darkness of the cell, but he knew he was there.

"Get up, you bastard. I can smell you and hear your breathing, so I know you're there," the man in the doorway said.

Thomas slowly shifted his weight under himself and, using his many years of experience in calming himself when he was afraid, said in a voice that belied the apprehension he felt, "Are you here to take me to see Guillaume de Nogaret? If not, I believe I will wait right here."

The man in the doorway said, "I don't know or care who I am taking you to see. I have been told to fetch you, and I will do so. I would rather not enter this filthy cave, but I will if I must. And you will be the sorrier for it. They didn't tell me I had to bring you alive, and one more dead Templar priest won't upset anyone."

Knowing he had no real choice, Thomas didn't say a word but walked forward to the doorway and the sunlight. He was hustled down several corridors he knew well, but somehow, the place felt different. In the past, the halls were often filled with Templar knights, squires, men-at-arms, clergy, and bookkeepers, all moving through with various tasks and responsibilities. Now, the King's men were standing about at multiple junctions and doors, mostly looking bored. Where the commandry had been meticulously clean and tidy, now trash and broken furnishings were scattered about. However, worse still, there was an awful smell. At first, Thomas recognized the odor of human waste, but there was something else Thomas wasn't familiar with. Later, he would come to know this aroma, and it would stick with him throughout the rest of his life; it was the smell of fear. It was a smell he would always associate with death, decay, and the loss of humanity, but mostly, it would be guilt that the odor made him feel.

Thomas was pushed along to the chapel by the man who had retrieved him from the cell. He was taken to the library, where a man in Cardinal robes sat at a desk looking over documents from the Paris Commandry. As soon as Thomas stood before the desk, the Cardinal looked up and said, "I am Cardinal Hugh, and you are Thomas, the priest?"

"Yes, your Eminence. I believe there has been a mistake. If you could talk to Guillaume de Nogaret, you would find that I should not be locked up."

The Cardinal stared at Thomas for a long moment. Then, as if Thomas hadn't spoken, he said, "I understand you were involved in providing information that may have aided the King in his arrests. But I was also told you were traveling with one of the Holy Relics that the Church would like to retrieve from this unholy Order for safekeeping and the Glory of God."

"I was traveling with a small group who were transporting some item the Grand Master valued, but I do not believe it was a Holy Relic," Thomas said. "They made me return to Paris when they realized something was going on and that they required more information."

"Why do you think the object is not a Holy Relic?"

Thomas had to think for a moment. His mind seemed to be working very slowly. Finally, he said, "I do not know for sure that the object is not a relic, but the way the Grand Master spoke of it made me believe it was not a holy item but rather a temporal one that he felt was of great value."

The Cardinal asked, "Do you know the route the group with the object is traveling?"   "Not exactly, but I know where it is headed; it should not be hard to send a few soldiers to retrieve it," Thomas said.

"Hum, 'not hard,' you say?"

"No, your Eminence. It is being taken to Rennes-le-Chateau."

The Cardinal looked at Thomas as if he were an idiot and said, "That region of France has proven to be less than helpful in our endeavor to crush your Order. For some reason, the seneschals and other judiciary functionaries have failed to locate a single member of the Templars in that region. It also appears that there are members of the clergy down there who, although they are not members of your Order, seem to be aiding the Templars. That region of France was a stronghold of the Cathars, and even after all these years since we cleansed the Earth of their vile heresy, they still corrupt those who live there."

Thomas quickly put in, "They are not 'my' Order, your Eminence. I was sent here by Guillaume de Nogaret to gather information. I only joined to get my ear closer to the leadership."

"Yes, I have been informed. Yet you did join the Order. Therefore, I do have some questions regarding your integrity, but that is another issue we will cover later. For the moment, I am only interested in the item you helped transport out of our reach."

Chapter 24

It was well after dark the following day when William, Sergeant Bertrand, and Louis arrived in Clermont. Bertrand was getting worse. He slept most of the time and had fitful dreams: he shook as though he was freezing, but sweat poured off him. He ate nothing and only sipped at the wine or water they offered him. The wound was festering and emitting a foul odor.

They rode straight to the tavern where William had first met Michael. Michael had them take the wagon with Bertrand to the stables behind the bar and went to get a few supplies. After he had looked at the wound by lantern light, he said to William, "It's bad. I'm not sure if I can reverse this. I have a room I sleep in next to these stables; we'll put him there, and I'll do what I can. Now help me with him."

William told Louis to stay with the wagon as he helped carry Bertrand to the room. After lying Bertrand on a pallet on the floor of the small room, Michael took a ceramic jar from the shelf. He told William, "I don't have much of this left and no way to get any more. I can't promise it will even help, but it's the best I can offer. It's mercuric chloride. The Islamic healers use it in the Holy Lands, and no one here knows how to make it. I'll try it if you like, but it'll not be cheap."

William said, "Do whatever you can. I'll pay the fee."

Michael said, "No offense, but as you are traveling through, I'll take that payment upfront. If your friend here dies and you decide to ride off, I'll be out my time, money, and my last bit of real medicine."

William opened a small satchel that hung from his sword belt and took out three gold coins. "Will this cover it?" he asked a bit harsher than he really felt.

"That'll do," Michael responded as if he hadn't noticed the tone.

William left and went back to the tavern. The place was a little warm, and many people were talking and laughing loudly. William ordered bread, roasted rabbit, pears, and cabbage. He told the man who ran the tavern, "My companion and I will be sleeping in the stable with our wagon." Holding another coin out to him, William asked, "Will this cover our expenses?"

The tavern owner took the coin, scrutinizing it carefully, and said, "Yes, this should be enough for the one night."

William knew that was enough for two or three days, but didn't feel like arguing. William gathered the food and returned to the stable. Neither William nor Louis had really eaten anything all day as they were so focused on reaching Clermont. William cut the rabbit in half and divided the other food between them. Louis was unusually quiet as he ate his food sparingly. William finally asked him, "What's wrong?"

Louis responded, "Will the Sergeant make it?"

"If God wills it, then yes, but if not… that is also God's will," William said.

"What will we do if he dies? Do we go back to the commandery?

William looked sharply at Louis and said, "No! The Grand Master of our Order has given us an assignment, and we must complete it, no matter what difficulties we face. Now, finish eating and get some sleep. I'll brush down the horses and keep watch first, then wake you."

The next morning, Louis woke William at first light and said, "A few hours ago, I started hearing voices from the room you took Sergeant Bertrand to. One of the voices seemed to be the Sergeant's. At first, it sounded like they were arguing, but then the voices calmed down. I haven't heard anything in the last hour or so."

William rose and said, "Wait here. I'll go over and see how things are with the Sergeant. Also, check all the horses thoroughly, as we still have several miles to cover before we reach Rennes-le-Chateau. I want to be ready as soon as the Sergeant has recovered."

Louis began to go to the first horse, Sergeant Bertrand's war horse. As he started inspecting the flanks of the horse, Louis said, just loud enough for William to hear as he left the stables, "If he recovers."

William entered the room where Michael had the Sergeant and saw that Michael was up, tending a small fire in a stove. The Sergeant seemed to be sleeping comfortably. Michael rose slowly as William entered. "How is he?" William asked, looking at Bertrand.

"It was a rough night; he still has a fever, and the wound still looks bad. I've burned away all the rotten flesh I can and have used about half of the small stock of mercuric chloride that I have left.

But, to answer your question, it's too early to tell," said Michael. After briefly pausing, he continued, "There is another matter we need to discuss."

"I believe I've already paid you enough, sir. I will not be fleeced just because you think me too young to know better," William said hotly.

"No, that's not it. You've paid me more than enough. What I need to discuss with you is a matter more delicate than money. I've suspected something since I first worked on your friend there in the wagon on the roadside. And after last night, I'm certain," Michael said.

"What are you going on about?" William asked, although he was confident he already knew.

"It's that you men are Templars," Michael said and waited for William to respond. William said nothing. He had no idea what to say. William knew it was important to conceal who they were, but this subterfuge was too new and too contrary to his way of thinking for him to be comfortable with it. He had no response, so he just stared at Michael with what he hoped was a look of dismay.

When Michael realized William was going to say nothing, he continued, "You don't need to worry about me. I went crusading as a younger man, partly to atone for a grievous ill I caused another and partly for adventure. I found neither atonement nor the type of adventure I had imagined I would find. However, I did know Templars and Hospitallers during my time there. Of all the soldiers for Christendom I encountered, they were the only ones who seemed to fight with honor.

"I once witnessed a single Templar ride off against thirty or more Saracens to aid a small group of pilgrims on foot that a group of mounted knights from England abandoned when the Saracens attacked. He knew he was going to die, but he rode on anyway. Arrows felled him before he could even reach the Saracens, and all the pilgrims were killed or captured. Yet I believe it was the greatest act of bravery I personally witnessed in my time there. I relayed this story to another Templar I knew and added that I didn't understand the knight's choice: giving up his life for such a hopeless cause. The Templar I spoke with replied, "As Templars, we give up our lives the moment we take our vows. It was not a choice he made at that moment after weighing the odds of success. He was submitting his will to a choice he made years earlier when he became a Templar. Not riding to the aid of pilgrims would have been breaking his vows. The odds or chance of success don't matter. Only duty and honor do."

"I have never met a Templar who did not display a deep commitment to your Rule. I've met some truly arrogant Templars, but none who would commit the heinous acts the King accuses your Order of. Your friend here has the marks of previous wounds, the likes of which I have only witnessed in Outremer. And you, by your bearing, can only be a knight. Yet, you display no coat of arms to indicate who your lord is. You are too formal and free with your money to be a free rider. And, in his delirium last night, your Sergeant confirmed what I already suspected."

William was still at a loss for what to say, but he knew he had to respond somehow. "And what do you plan on doing with this information?" was all that came to mind.

"I only mean to warn you to be very careful. Although many men in this part of France hold little love for Philip the Beautiful, sitting in his palace in Paris. Yet if the Pope were to get behind the arrests, many would feel it was their sacred duty to see all Templars arrested and sent to Paris, or just killed. Even now, many here would hand you over to the King's men in the hopes of receiving a reward. I would advise you to keep out of sight as much as possible and hold a little tighter to your purse strings."

Chapter 25

Garrard and Henry sat in silence in their cell for some time. Henry wasn't sure if Garrard could even speak with so many teeth removed. Finally, Henry asked, "Why do you think they locked us up separately from the others?"

Garrard looked at Henry momentarily and said with difficulty, "Because we opposed them. They don't want our defiance to spread."

Henry said, "This is all so unbelievable. Where is Grand Master Jacques de Molay? I don't understand. Who has accused us? Why hasn't the Pope intervened on our behalf? Why are our brother knights so craven that they are just confessing to whatever they are accused of?"

Apparently not in a talking mood, Garrard looked at Henry and slowly shook his head as if to say he had no answers. Henry said, "We should demand to see the Grand Master or rally the brothers and stop this foolishness. If we all charged at once, they could not oppose us."

"Maybe that is another reason you and I sit in this cell, Sir Henry," Garrard replied.

And sit there they did. The two had no idea how long they had been left in the cell, as there was no window or any other means to determine the passage of time. Food and water were given to them infrequently through a small hatch in their door. No one responded to their inquiries or protestations. The chamber pot in the cell was never taken out to be emptied, so their waste was piled in the corner of the room. At first, they talked to each other. As hunger and the deterioration of their mental and emotional statuses took hold, speaking became a chore they preferred to skip.

Then, one day, the door opened. They could see three men standing in the hallway beyond. One of the men said, "Get up, scum. You have a meeting to attend, and we need to wash some of that smell off you first." Neither Garrard nor Henry moved or spoke, partly because they were still trying to process the fact that the door was wide open, and because they were unsure they could get their legs working to stand up.

Another of the three said, "Maybe they're dead."

The man who initially spoke said, "At least one of them is alive. I can hear him breathing. Are you two coming, or should we close this door and not open it again until the stench of your rotted corpses forces us to?"

Henry slowly started to rise. As he did, he took Garrard's arm to help him to his feet. They stood still for a moment, trying to get their balance, then took an uncertain step toward the door. By working together, they leaned on one another, kept their feet, and began moving forward. They were led down the hallway and out to the practice yard. Once there, the guard who was in charge said, "Strip." Both Garrard and Henry were already shivering, but they complied with the command. Once they were naked, the other two guards dumped several buckets of frigid water on them both. After this, they were given rough, spun robs like those of a novice monk. Then, they were taken to a room where three men, one wearing Cardinal robes, sat behind a desk.

The Cardinal asked, "You are Sir Garrard de Paris and Sir Henry de Creon?"

Both Henry and Garrard nodded: "Yes, your eminence."

"I wish to inform you that I am not here as a subject of King Philip. I am here at the request of the Holy Father to consider the validity of the accusations against your Order. According to the records we have been provided, you two did not confess to any of the crimes committed by your Order. You may be interested to know that you are in the minority. Most of your brothers, including your Grand Master, have confessed to a number of disturbing acts."

Both Henry and Garrard just stood there, not knowing what to say. Neither could believe Grand Master Jacques de Molay would betray the Templars. The Cardinal continued to stare at them, not saying a word. Finally, as if concluding his inner struggles, Garrard stood a little straighter and said, "Your Eminence, I cannot speak for other men, but I have been a Knight Templar for over twenty years. I have never been involved in, nor have I witnessed any of the vile acts we have been accused of."

"And you, Sir Henry?" the Cardinal asked.

Henry replied, "Nor I, your Eminence. I also find it hard to believe that any of my brothers have either. It was the torture that made them confess."

The Cardinal looked more closely at Henry and said, "So they are guilty of presenting falsehoods to a representative of the Church?"

"When some men are being tortured, they can lose all sense of who they are. They are good men and good Christians, but the pain and fear broke them. Fear can weigh on a man's soul to the point where it is crushed. I was in that room for many days, repeatedly witnessing fellow brothers being tortured before they chose to ask me a single question. One man I witnessed had his feet burned so badly that the bones fell out of the stubs his feet had become. It wasn't until that point that he confessed to crimes they had repeatedly accused him of and that he had previously repeatedly denied," Garrard said.

"Yet you two did not confess. I find it hard to believe the brave men of the Knights Templar are so craven as to perjure themselves due to a little pain and fear. These are the men who had won the Holy Lands for us. Or is it, as the people say, are you only the faint image of the men who won the Holy Lands? Should you more accurately be called the men who lost the most holy sites in the world?" the Cardinal asked.

Neither Garrard nor Henry had a response, so they quietly stood looking at the ground before the table where the Cardinal sat.

The Cardinal, realizing there would be no answer, said, "Well, let us proceed." Looking to the man on his left, he said, "Charles, please record our discussion for the Holy Father." Then, looking back at the men before him, he said, "Sir Garrard de Paris and Sir Henry de Creon, have you ever spat or urinated on the Cross, denied Christ, committed acts of homosexuality with fellow brothers, or been involved in idol worship?"

Both men raised their eyes up from the floor and looked directly at the Cardinal as they said, "No, your Eminence."

After a brief pause, the Cardinal asked, "Have you ever witnessed such acts, or do you know anything about clandestine meetings where such acts took place?"

"No, your Eminence," both men said in unison.

The Cardinal continued, "Do you know anything about Holy Relics being taken away to places of hiding by your Order?"

Garrard said, "No, your Eminence." But Henry did not speak.

116

The Cardinal raised an eyebrow and, looking at Henry, said, "And you, Sir Henry?"   "I'm not certain how to answer, Your Eminence. Shortly before the arrests, I was asked by the Grand Master to escort something to a town in Southern France. I do not know what the item is because it was sealed in a crate, and we were instructed not to open it. But there was some discussion among our group that it might be a Holy Relic that the Order was keeping secret," Henry said while returning his gaze to the ground.

"You did not find it odd that you were asked not to look in the crate? Obviously, someone was hiding something," the Cardinal said.

Henry looked up at the Cardinal again: "No, your Eminence. If I am given an order, I obey it. I do not find it odd that the Grand Master elected not to keep me in his confidence, as I am one of many brothers he calls on to perform various tasks. He does not need to explain anything to any of us. We are sworn to obey all commands of the Grand Master as if the Pope himself gave the order."

The Cardinal, somewhat angered by Henry's arrogant tone, said, "It would seem many things went on in secret within your Order. Maybe idolatry and homosexuality were common practices behind closed doors within your commanderies."

"That is a lie! And I will challenge any man to face me with a sword if he accuses me of such acts!" Henry said before he could stop himself.

The Cardinal turned nearly as red as his robes and rose from his chair, "You had better watch your tongue, young sir! You are close to threatening a representative of the Church and, therefore, the Holy Father himself. By doing so, you challenge the very will of God! You keep such threats to yourself. You will answer our questions, and that is all. Am I clear?"

Henry fixed his eyes on the Cardinal's a moment longer, then lowered them and said, "I beg your pardon, your Eminence. I spoke without thought."

There was a pause as the tension hung in the air like a coming storm. Then the Cardinal sat down and said, "That is better. Now, what can you tell me about this crate you were delivering, and exactly where were you taking it?"

Henry said, "I really don't know what was in the crate. The crate itself was about six feet long, three feet wide, and three feet high. It appeared to be heavy, although I never lifted it. It was wrapped in a tarpaulin and chained closed. We were headed to a town called Rennes-le-Chateau."

"And did you deliver this crate?" the Cardinal asked.

"No. We decided to split up after we ran into some angry commoners and a seneschal who wished to arrest us for heresy. My squire, a priest named Thomas, a young lady whom we were protecting, and I returned to Paris. While Sir William de Sevrey, a Sergeant-at-arms, Bertrand, and William's squire, Louis, continued to Rennes-le-Chateau with the wagon and crate."

"What happened to the seneschal and the good citizens who tried to arrest you?"

"We were under orders by the Grand Master not to give up possession of the item in the crate, and they decided to attack us and take the crate. We were forced to fight them. The seneschal and a few others were killed," Henry responded.

"I see. So, you opposed a man who was carrying out orders from the King of France and some citizens who attempted to help him. You murdered them?" asked the Cardinal.

"It was not murder. We had no choice. The wagon with the crate would have been lost, and we had been ordered to protect it. We are the Knights Templar and are not subject to the laws of earthly monarchs. We answer only to the leaders in our Order and the Pope himself," said Henry.

"That may be in dispute, but let us continue. Were there any rumors about what was in the crate? Surely, you guessed at what was in it. Perhaps someone took a quick look?" the Cardinal asked.

Henry replied, "No one opened the crate while I was traveling with the wagon. Yes, there was some guessing, but mostly from William's squire, Louis. But it was just a way to fill the silence. There was nothing to it."

The Cardinal said, "Sometimes there is more to wild guessing than you might think. Indulge us. What were some of these guesses?"

Henry thought a moment, "I wasn't really paying a lot of attention. Louis seemed to talk constantly, so I mostly tried to ignore him. I recall him saying that it was possibly gold or relics. I believe he also mentioned it might be a bust of Grand Master Jacques de Molay. Like I said, it was just talk; there was nothing to it."

"Were there any particular relics that the young squire mentioned it could be?" the Cardinal asked.

Henry replied, "I know he mentioned a piece of the True Cross, the Ark of the Covenant, and the sword of St. Peter. I can't recall anything else."

The Cardinal then asked Henry, "What about this girl you mentioned? I wasn't aware the Templars sent women along on Templar business."

Henry was hoping the topic of Mary would not be brought up, and he almost didn't mention her, but felt it was better to be forthcoming at this juncture. "The girl was not with us originally. We came across some men who were attempting to rape her. We had only intended to take her as far as Vézelay, but that is where we encountered trouble. So, she stayed with us since the townspeople had already seen her in our company. When we decided to split up, it was determined that she should return to Paris with us."

"And what became of this girl?" the Cardinal asked.

"I don't know. I was knocked unconscious when we were arrested and have not seen or heard anything about my companions since that time," Henry replied.

Chapter 26

Mary woke with a start. She had been dreaming, but couldn't recall any details from the dream. Odo had been in the dream, as had a man in a long red robe and pointy hat who Mary assumed was a Cardinal in the Church. However, the robe and hat were not like any Cardinal she had ever seen. That was all Mary could remember besides the helplessness she felt upon waking. As she became aware of her surroundings, she recalled the events of earlier in the day. Darrick was no longer in the room, but there was still the smell of food from the kettle. Although the fire had burned down a little, there was still enough light to see.

Mary got up slowly. She had a headache and had cuts and bruises all over her body. She went to the kettle and looked inside: there was still stew in it, and it looked like fresh meat had been added, but it was not quite fully cooked. Mary was about to get some more when she heard someone coming inside. She moved further from the door and faced it. It was Darrick carrying a bucket of water. He went to the table he had butchered the deer on and dumped the water on the table, rinsing most of the blood onto the dirt floor. Then, he walked back out, never acknowledging Mary's presence.

At first, Mary was dumbfounded, then angry. She had often been treated as a nobody by people of higher standing than she, but this man was no better. What right did he have to ignore her? She stormed through the doorway along the bramble and vine tunnel with the intent of giving him a piece of her mind. As she stepped out into the afternoon sunlight and looked around, he was nowhere to be seen. She turned in a circle, looking for any sign of him. As she gazed about, she began to see the beauty of the woods for the first time. It was quiet, bright, and colorful in a way that human towns, cities, and even the great cathedrals could never duplicate. As she stood there taking it all in, she noticed movement out of the corner of her eye and turned. It was Derrick. He was carrying the same bucket, now refilled with water. Before she could say a word, he ducked back into the dwelling. She heard water splashing, presumably on the table. Once again, Derrick came out. She stepped in front of him and made him stop. "Are you just going to ignore me?"

Derrick looked her in the eyes, noting how pretty they were: "I'm not ignoring you. I'm getting chores done. And, right now, I'm going to get you some fresh water so you can clean your wounds. I have a poultice that you can apply to them. It might help with the itching."

Mary was also looking into his eyes and said, "Oh… sorry." Then she brightened a bit and said, "I'll come with you."

Derrick didn't respond but moved around her to head back into the woods. As Mary followed him into the trees, she began to hear water running over rocks. She noticed that steps had been cut into the ground, making navigation of the terrain easier as they descended toward the stream. The stream turned out to be quite broad, almost a river. The water seemed to flow out of the ground, running over a shallow rocky stream bed for forty or fifty feet and emptying into a broad pool. It then continued over more rocks downstream. There were large rocks, many of which were smooth on top, along the water's edge.

While Derrick refilled the bucket from the rocky stream, Mary went to the pool, took off her shoes, and sat on one of the large rocks. Dangling her feet into the water, she said with a sigh of contentment, "This is heavenly. It's so beautiful and peaceful, and the water feels so good on my feet." Derrick didn't respond, so she continued, "Can I get in the water and clean myself and my clothes? How deep is it? I can't swim," she added.

Darrick said, "It's not too deep, maybe up to your waist." Darrick had barely finished before Mary pushed herself off the rock into the water. She walked further into the pool until the water was above her legs and then sat down, plunging her head under. When she raised her head out of the water, she laughed. Derrick thought it was a pleasant sound.

Mary turned to Darrick and said, "Would you mind walking up into the woods a bit, but not so far you wouldn't hear me, so I can bathe and wash my clothes? I don't want to be alone, but I'd like to be able to remove my dress."

Darrick simply said, "Yes." And walked back into the woods, sitting behind a large tree trunk, facing away from the splashing sounds. He wondered how he would tell Mary that he planned to take her to the outskirts of Paris and leave her there. This morning, she was an inconvenience he had to deal with, but now…well…now he didn't know what she was. He sat there wondering what to do. For possibly the first time in his life, someone snuck up on him.

"There you are," Mary said, coming around the side of the tree. Darrick looked up and saw her standing over him. Her black hair was still wet and pulled back, and her dress was also wet and clung to her in a rather pleasant manner. She quickly moved off before Darrick could get to his feet. He caught up with her just as she reached the clearing outside his dwelling. She said, "I was going to leave my dress on the rock to dry, but although it felt wonderful to get in the water and get that grime off me, I soon realized the water was too cold to stay in any longer. I guess I'll sit out here in the sun and dry off." She sat on a log and closed her eyes while she faced the sun.

Darrick stood there for a moment, unsure of what to do. Then, he decided to get the poultice for her many scrapes and cuts. Darrick set the bucket of water just outside the doorway as he entered. As the coolness of the dwelling washed over him, causing him to shiver, Darrick realized he was warm and a little shaky, similar to how he felt a few months ago after killing a wolf that had nearly attacked him before he got an arrow in it. Darrick sat on the edge of the table for a moment and forced himself to calm down. Just then, he heard a scream from outside. He quickly grabbed his bow and three arrows, which he always left leaning by the doorway as he hurried outside.

Mary was on her feet and backing toward him with her eyes fixed on the log. Darrick looked where she was staring and almost laughed. He said, "It's alright, she won't hurt you. Unless you frighten her, and even then, she probably won't injure you, but you'll regret it all the same. It's just close to her dinner time."

As Darrick said this, the skunk climbed up on a log, looking at them both. Darrick ducked back through the doorway, deposited his bow and arrows in their customary location, and retrieved the gizzard from the deer he had set aside. Returning outside, he walked up to the log and held the gizzard above the skunk so that it had to stand on its hind legs to reach it. Darrick stepped back a little and turned to look back at Mary, and said, "It's best to keep a little distance from animals while they eat, even friendly ones such as Bernadette here."

"Bernadette?" Mary asked. "She's a pet of yours?"

Darrick replied, "No, not a pet. She's a wild animal who comes by for a meal most evenings and sometimes sits with me for a bit before she goes off on her nightly adventures."

The skunk had quickly devoured the gizzard and now licked her paws. Darrick moved back to the log and sat beside her, stroking her black and white coat. Mary moved closer and slowly sat on the other side of the skunk. "May I?" she asked.

Darrick stopped petting the animal, and Mary cautiously reached out, carefully running her hand across Bernadette's thick fur. "Aren't you worried she'll spray you?" Mary asked.

"No, she's been coming here for some time. At first, I would just see her eyes in the woods as she watched me, and I watched her. Then I started tossing her little morsels of food, not too much, just enough to coax her out, as I didn't want her dependent on me to feed her. That's a quick way to doom an animal. Over the next month or so, I slowly tossed the food closer to myself until I got her to accept it from my hand. One night, she jumped up on this log after I gave her a bit of meat, and she let me pet her."

Bernadette suddenly jumped down and waddled away toward the woods. "She never stays long," Darrick said. "It's probably not a good thing that she's gotten comfortable with humans. I hope it doesn't get her killed one day."

As Mary watched the feline form disappear into the trees, she asked, "Why'd you name her Bernadette? An old girlfriend?"

Darrick didn't respond for a minute. He'd never actually thought about it. Darrick had just started calling her that one day while trying to draw her closer. "I guess because that was my sister's name," he finally replied.

Mary noted the hint of sadness in his response and, feeling it would be an intrusion on this private man's life, she decided not to ask. Instead, she rested the hand that she had used to pet Bernadette upon his hand. Darrick reacted as though Mary had pinched him. He quickly pulled his hand away and stood up. He walked toward the dwelling and disappeared inside before she could offer an apology. Soon, he came back out with a small clay jar in his hands. He strode up to her, handed her the ointment, and said, "Apply this to your scratches. It'll help them heal." He then walked over beside the dwelling and removed some boards which had covered a hole in the ground.

He began cooking some meat over the campfire he had built up outside the hut. Mary approached him and said, "Thanks for the poultice; what is in it?"

"Bear grease and some herbs; a woodcutter showed me how to make it," he replied.

After a brief silence, Mary said, "I'm sorry if I intruded back there."

Darrick sighed, "You did nothing wrong. I'm just not used to being touched, and I overreacted. Maybe I've lived out here too long to be around people."

Mary wanted to say something, but really had no idea how to respond, so she just sat there watching the fire and listening to meat sizzle. After several moments, she said, "That smells really good."

With more life in his voice now that the topic had changed, Darrick said, "It's the backstrap from the deer I got earlier today. It's the best part, and other than a few pieces I put fresh in the stew pot and some of the organs, it's the only part I don't smoke. There's a small, shallow cave just over there that I smoke meat in. I closed it up with large rocks and some logs."

After a brief silence, Mary said, "You've never really asked me what I was doing in the woods, where I was going, or really anything about myself."

Not thinking about it, Darrick said, "I assumed you're from Paris. I figured tomorrow I'll take you back close enough that you could see the city and leave you to walk home."

Mary suddenly grew angry and retorted, "You 'assumed' and you 'figured' incorrectly. I'm not going back to the city. There's no home for me there."

Again, unsure what had just happened, Darrick said, "Where is your home? I'll take you there."

Mary said, "I don't have a home. I need to get to Rennes-le-Chateau."

Not understanding how he had somehow offended her, Darrick said, "Ok, I'll take you there. Where is that?"

Chapter 27

Odo knew he was getting weaker in body, mind, and spirit and needed to escape the squalid environment soon. He didn't know what to try next. It would have been easier if they had been asked questions or told something, but sitting and doing nothing, knowing nothing, was beginning to weigh on Odo's mind. He started to become paranoid, thinking the others were secretly talking about him. He could almost hear them saying, "Fool thought he could just walk out the door. He was off on a secret mission for the Grand Master, probably what got us all locked up." The other men noticed his change in demeanor: how he would look at them sharply as in a rage and then look away, grumbling to himself. They realized he was going mad and chose to keep their distance, isolating his disturbed mind even further.

Odo had moments of clear lucidity when he realized he no longer thought as he used to. He wondered if the blow to his head from the guard had injured his way of thinking. However, these moments became briefer and further apart as time passed. At one point, he was sure he heard two men talking about someone named "Baphomet" who would rescue them. He recalled hearing stories of Baphomet, or perhaps it was Baphometh, from some of the old crusading monks. Sometimes, it seemed the old crusaders were referring to a group of people. Other times, it seemed they were talking about a demon.

Later that night, as he tried to sleep, he had a dream in which a creature walked upright like a man but had the head and hooves of a goat. The beast spoke to him in a language Odo did not recognize. He suddenly woke to the sounds of screaming; it was a long, insane scream. Odo realized in an instant that it was he who was screaming. At that moment, he knew that the creature he saw in his dream was Baphomet and that Baphomet had been sent into his dreams by some of the men around him, his fellow Templars. Odo also knew that Baphomet intended to kill him in his sleep. He had a moment of divine clarity where he knew, without a shadow of a doubt, that Baphomet was the root of all the sins that had permeated the Templars. He had to tell someone before Baphomet could kill him. The only possible protection from this demon was the Church. He knew he must get help. Odo leapt to his feet, dashed to the door, and began pounding on it, screaming, "You must let me see a priest. I know what is causing the evil that has brought this Order to the gates of Hell."

The guards at the door were caught by surprise as this crazy man ran to the door and began pounding and screaming. One of the guards looked at his partner, shrugged, and approached Odo from behind with the intent of shutting this crazy Templar up for good. But just then, the door was unlocked and opened from the outside. The door was opened only a few inches before Odo pushed it with all his might and slipped through. He ran headlong into two other guards who grabbed hold of him before he could continue his flight. Odo was still yelling, "It's Baphomet! They've sent him to kill me since I know the secret. You must take me to a priest before it's too late."

Suddenly, another man standing behind the guards said, "What is it, my son? What are you talking about?"

Odo made eye contact with the man who spoke to him and recognized him as a member of the clergy. Odo said, "It's the demon, Baphomet. That's who the knights have been worshiping, and even now, some of his agents are trying to send him to kill me since I discovered their blasphemy."

The priest spoke to the guards holding Odo and said, "Bring him." Then he turned and walked briskly away.

Odo was nearly dragged by the two guards as they tried to keep up with the priest. Eventually, the priest came to a stop before a large oak door. He turned and said to the guards, "Wait here." Then he opened the door, entered, and closed the door behind him.

While Odo waited before the door, still being held by the guards, he began to talk to himself: "It all makes sense now. Late-night secret meetings with only the knights allowed in… a Templar outside the door with a drawn sword… they must be forcing the new knights to worship Baphomet! Then, there's the secret coded language only a few know. They say it's so they can handle money transactions privately, but it's just part of their hidden agenda. That must be why we lost against the Muslims. The leadership of the Templars must have been in league with the Devil. Baphomet is the Devil's agent!" Then he turned and started pleading with the guard on his right, "You must help me. I need to see a priest or some clergy; otherwise, Baphomet will kill me where I stand. He can reach me anywhere. Only the Church can help me."

The guards, who had been listening to his ramblings, were somewhat nervous that this clearly unstable man would speak to them. At the same time, the things he was talking about frightened them. The two guards looked at each other, then, without saying a word, chose just to ignore him and stared straight ahead at the closed door before them. Soon, but not too soon for the guards, the priest opened the door and said, "Bring him in." The two guards entered the room and released the now incoherently whimpering man before a large table with three stern-looking monks seated behind it. The priest told them, "You are excused. Wait for me outside." The two guards happily complied.

Odo looked up and, seeing the three monks, cried out, "You must help me. He's coming for me. I don't know how to protect myself. They mean to have me killed since I have discovered the truth. Please protect me."

"Who is coming for you?" the monk on the right asked.

"Baphomet!" Odo nearly shrieked in fear.

"And who is Baphomet? Is he one of the knights? If so, trust me, he will not harm you."

"No, Baphomet is the demon that the Knights of the Temple worship. It is Baphomet who has caused us to lose the Holy Lands. I didn't know anything about it, but I heard two of the men who were being held with me talking about the creature. When they noticed me listening, they worked their evil and sent him to kill me. I saw him in a dream, and I realized…I just knew who he was and that he was the demon the knights worshiped. It all makes sense now: those secret meetings, secret codes, all of it. That is the foul evil that permeates this place. Can't you feel it even now? Baphomet has power here. The Grand Master is in league with a creature of Hell. He has made all the other knights swear oaths, disgusting oaths, to Baphomet. You must help me! I need your protection." Odo brought his hands to his face and began to weep.

The three monks looked at each other. The one in the middle spoke for the first time. "My son, we have been sent by the Church to look over the records and aid in the search for the money that the Templars have here. We are not involved in the matters you speak of, but I will have you taken to the brothers who are conducting that investigation. No doubt they will want to speak to you about this Baphomet. But before they speak to you, since you are cleansing your soul, do you know where the Templars kept their money? We know they must have great wealth stored here, yet we've found nothing."

Odo didn't seem to have heard. He just kept on weeping. The middle monk looked at the priest who brought Odo to them and said, "He's of no use to us. He's obviously gone mad. Have the king's men take him to The Citadel and to the Inquisition. Perhaps they'll find his babblings useful."

Chapter 28

Thomas' situation had improved somewhat. He was no longer locked in a cell. He was allowed to eat regular meals with the other clergy, but he was not permitted to leave the commandery. He had even been given a job. He was to go through the records and help determine the location of all the assets that the Templars held throughout France and try to determine their approximate value.

While going about his assigned task Father Thomas learned that all the leadership of the Templars, all the common knights, and most of the sergeants who had been caught had been taken to the dungeons under the castle in Paris. A select few knights who were of higher value to the King of France were being held separately in a undisclosed location.

In addition, anyone involved with the management of the fleet, lands, and money of the Templars had also been taken to the castle dungeons. All the support personnel, such as squires, blacksmiths, farmers, and carpenters, were being kept in the various commanderies around France until someone could decide what to do with them. As for the clergy of the Templars, there seemed to be no one place that they had been taken. Some, like himself, were being held at the commanderies. Some had been brought to the castle. No one knew what had happened to others who had escaped capture.

Thomas wondered what had become of Sir Henry and Odo. He even pondered about the vixen Mary; had she made good her escape? But mostly, he speculated about where the other group was. Surely, they couldn't have reached Rennes-le-Chateau yet, even if they had evaded capture. He'd love to see that Sergeant Bertrand gets what he deserves. He wished he had found out what was in the crate. The Grand Master only told him enough so that Thomas knew it had to be a significant object, not just the supposed finger bone of some saint no one had ever heard of. He had been told that as soon as they arrived in Rennes-le-Chateau, he was to meet with Father Lull and that Father Lull was going to introduce him to a "great secret of the Templars."

But he had no idea what that secret was or even what it related to. He assumed it had to do with whatever was in the crate, but he didn't really know. He had been studying the history of the Templars for months before they left for Rennes-le-Chateau in the hopes that it might reveal something. Most of what he read was common knowledge.

The Templars rose from nine knights to Europe's most powerful standing army, a multi-national trade organization, and the first international banking system. They amassed great wealth, initially through gifts of money and land, and later through the wise use of these assets. They developed a vast fleet of ships to transport their supplies to the Holy Lands, and, for a price, they would provide passage for pilgrims. They then shipped goods back to Europe on the now mostly empty fleet. Goods that were actively sought after, such as sugar in both its regular granular form and as sugar dissolved in boiling water and then allowed to dry into crystals, which the Arabs called al-Kandiq and the Europeans called candy. They carried fine cotton cloth, which those in Europe greatly desired as they were accustomed to clothes made of much more cumbersome leather and coarse wool.

With all these enterprises, they accumulated more money and began to move into banking. Initially, they stored and protected the wealth and possessions of the wealthy. This was a natural application of their situation. What better location to keep money than trusting it to the secure vaults in a local Templar commandery guarded by warrior monks who had taken a vow of poverty? Of course, there was always a donation to the Templars for providing such a service. Even the crown jewels of France and England were, at times, given to the Knights Templar for safekeeping.

Later, their banking activities grew. If someone needed to borrow money, the Templars would help. However, since charging interest was against Church law, none was charged, although gifts of various types were welcomed. If no donation was available upfront, the Templars could choose to receive most of the profits produced by the farm, mill, or other business for which the individual wanted to borrow the money for a set number of years. If the business venture failed altogether, the Templars would acquire all the land and assets associated with the business. At the time of the Templars' arrest, the Crown of France was deeply indebted to the Templars, having borrowed a substantial amount of money over the preceding few years to support its military campaigns.

Additionally, since the Templars had commanderies throughout Europe and the Holy Land, they devised the most effective way to travel safely with money. Individuals could deposit money in one location, where they were given a sealed note. When the traveler arrived at their destination, they presented the sealed letter and could withdraw money from the commandry there. The funds would be converted to the appropriate currency for an added fee. To facilitate this and ensure that an individual didn't cheat by claiming to have deposited more money in France than they had, the Templars developed codes that only they knew how to read. The code revealed the depositor's identity, the amount deposited, and the currency used. Again, all this was done for a donation to the cause.

Although Thomas knew the Templars were involved in various enterprises, he did not realize the scope or diversity of operations that the Templars oversaw until he began to review their books. There were vast tracts of land for farming, mills, stone quarries, horse breeding, carpentry shops, storage facilities, tanneries, and the list went on. This did not include the operations connected to the business of training and maintaining an army, such as blacksmith shops, stables, and shipbuilding.

He found no reference to where money, gold, or any other purely monetary items were kept. There was no mention of currency loaned or paid back to the Templars in any of the books he went through. It still puzzled him that in all the time he had spent at the commandery in Paris, he still had no idea where the money was kept. He never saw anyone transporting funds or knew of any rooms with special guards posted or more restrictions than any other areas. But surely, with this being the primary commandery in France, they had to keep some money here.

Thomas walked to Cardinal Hugh's office to seek an audience. As he was walking the corridor, he saw Cardinal Hugh and two priests approaching from the other end. When Cardinal Hugh saw him, he said, "Thomas, exactly the man I wanted to speak to. Come to my office. We have a matter to discuss."

The Cardinal seemed in a good mood, and although Thomas had met with him a few times, he wasn't sure how to judge if this good mood was a good or bad situation for him. He entered the office with some unease, following the Cardinal and the other two priests.

Thomas waited in front of the desk until the Cardinal had seated himself. The Cardinal looked at Thomas and said, "It appears you may be of more use to us than we thought. But before we get into that, I need to know what you know about Baphomet?"

Thomas got a confused look on his face and said, "I'm sorry, Your Eminence, but I don't know what that is."

The Cardinal got a hard look in his eyes and said in a cold voice, "Think carefully. Have you ever heard anyone speak of Baphomet?"

Thomas swallowed, not liking the sound of this. In as steady a voice as Thomas could maintain, he said, "I'm sorry, but I have never heard that word before."

"I suppose it's just as well you haven't. Baphomet appears to be a creature from Hell and may be at the core of all the evil pervading the Templar Order." The Cardinal paused to see what reaction this might cause in Thomas.

Thomas was both stunned and pleased by this statement. He was pleased because, for the first time, the Cardinal talked to Thomas about the Templars and did not refer to them as "your Order." "If I may ask, Your Eminence, how was this discovered, and what do we know of this creature?" Thomas said.

The Cardinal looked to the priest who stood on his right and said, "This is Brother Jaye of the Holy Inquisition. He has come here to speak to you about exactly those questions. Brother Jaye…"

Thomas had to strain to hear Brother Jaye partly because the brother spoke in a quiet, almost timid voice, but mostly because of the roaring in his ears produced by his fear of the Inquisition.

Brother Jaye said, "It was a man we believe you are acquainted with who has brought the creature Baphomet to our attention. A squire named Odo. He has become a bit unhinged due to his fear of Baphomet, and his minions are difficult to comprehend. But he mentioned your name and asked if he could speak with you. At first, we thought that he was implicating you in the worship of this unholy creature, but, upon further questioning, we discovered that he believes you are a true man of God, and he can trust you."

Thomas was stunned by this revelation, and it took him a moment to realize they were waiting for him to speak. Finally, he stammered, "I am taken aback by this. Yes, I know Odo and will gladly do all I can to help uncover this evil in our midst."

The Cardinal said, "Good, you are to leave for the castle with Brother Jaye immediately."

Chapter 29

William was trying to sleep in the wagon while Louis walked around the barn, trying to stay awake and alert. William might have been able to sleep if all Louis did was walk. But Louis would occasionally start humming or mumbling to himself, talking to one of the horses, or picking up a stick and tapping it on the floor or wall as he walked. They had been in Clermont for five days. Sergeant Bertrand was doing better but was not yet well enough to ride a horse or even rise from his pallet. Michael had told William just this evening that the Sergeant's fever was returning. Since he had no more real medicine to give, the Sergeant's recovery was up to Bertrand and God. William had tried to speak to Bertrand, but the Sergeant kept drifting off to sleep during the conversation. William really did not know what to do. They could not stay here forever. He had a mission to complete, yet he didn't relish the idea of leaving without the Sergeant.

The door to the stables creaked open, and William instantly rose, sword in hand. He was pleased to see Louis was also moving toward the wagon with William's warhammer raised and ready for action. Since they had lots of time on their hands, William had resumed training Louis in the use of sword and shield. They also practiced with the warhammer and dagger. Louis had always been good at practicing with weapons, but after recent events, he took it more seriously and was becoming a more formidable match for William. Recently, Louis began carrying the warhammer while on guard duty.

Michael stepped into the stable, closed the door behind him, and said in a near whisper, "Get your team hitched up and get loaded. You two need to be out of town as soon as possible."

William lowered his sword and said, "What are you talking about? What about Sergeant Bertrand? We can't just leave him. What has happened?"

"You shouldn't be worried about the Sergeant. He's the one who sent me over here; he wants you to start getting ready to leave immediately. But before you depart, he wants you, William, to speak to him. There are rumors that Jacques de Molay has confessed to heresy, buggery, and demon worship. There are men in town who have started to talk about you three and their suspicions that you are

Templars hiding from the King. As we speak, they are drinking to build up their courage and slow their wits. Before too many hours, you are going to have a mob in here trying to take you prisoner or worse. The Sergeant cannot be moved. I don't like his chances as it is, but if you try to take him with you, he will not only slow you down, but he will surely die. I'll protect him if I can, but in his present state, I don't think they would hurt him…outright, at least. But you two will likely end up dead along with several drunk men from Clermont, and whatever you have there in the wagon will be taken."

William said, "Louis, start hitching the mules to the wagon, prepare the horses, and get things ready to go. Michael, please take me to Bertrand."

William and Michael left the stables as Louis quickly began harnessing the mules. Before they entered the room where Sergeant Bertrand was, Michael said, "He's weak but mostly lucid, at least when I left."

William entered the room and went immediately to the Sergeant's bedside. Bertrand looked William in the eyes and said, "You two need to be on the move as soon as possible, but before you go, I want to tell you a few things. I want you to listen and not argue. First, when you leave, take all my gear; leave nothing behind. I believe we, as an Order, are in for some very challenging times. You may be called on to do things well beyond your experience and knowledge. You were chosen for this mission for a reason. When the Grand Master decided to assemble this small group, he came to me and asked who I thought could best lead this mission. I gave him your name. I have watched you around the commandery for a while now, and I believe you have what it takes to be a leader. Most knights are followers and can't think beyond their next meal. But all that thinking you do can get you into trouble. I'm going to boil down my thirty years of being a soldier into a few minutes of advice.

"Your brothers' lives are more important than your enemy's lives. You'll understand if you get into a sustained battle or war that lasts for weeks, months, or years. Once you see one of your brothers die, you will want revenge. Even killing ten or a hundred of the enemy won't matter as much to you as that one brother's death, at least not at the time. Later, you may feel differently. But if you fight to seek revenge, it will eat you alive. It will never end. There needs to be a clear goal and a specific method for achieving what you are trying to accomplish. If the fighting becomes killing just for the sake of killing, it serves little purpose.

"When you are with your fellow brothers, whether they are knights like yourself, or men-at-arms and squires, or a group of farmers you have banded together, you can never admit that you are afraid, no matter how frightened you are. You can never let them see fear in you. You can say you're concerned, anxious, excited, or even worried, but never fearful. Fear will kill an army faster than any enemy you face.

"A good leader likes to be in control. He never wants someone else to dictate what he should do next. But most soldiers, even the best warriors, are not good leaders in the heat of a fight; they cannot see beyond the tip of their weapons. Most need to be told what to do and how to do it. You are a leader, which means you need to make decisions and give commands. You must listen to those under you because they may know things you know nothing about or have a perspective you failed to notice. However, you still must make the final decisions, give the orders, and lead your men.

"In the midst of a battle, soldiers fight for themselves and their brothers around them. Little else matters. As a commander, you need to keep the bigger picture in mind. In the short term, the bigger picture may just be the battle, but you must also consider the broader objectives of the war. In the end, your true calling is often to fight for and protect the mindless, annoying individuals who have no idea they've put you in harm's way. These individuals can be commanders over you, pilgrims you're supposed to protect, even the general populace of France, all of Christendom, or possibly even the world's masses. Even if you reach a point where you don't care about the Templars as an organization or the individuals you are sworn to protect, you still must put your life on the line to serve them.

"Lastly, do not be over-trusting of other men. Many men out there will kill for a copper coin but will never work an honest day for a bag of gold. I'm tired now, so get out of here and get as far from this town as you can as quickly as possible. And get someone to knight that annoying, talkative squire of yours soon. He's too smart for his own good and needs the added responsibility to force him to grow up. Give him my arms and armor and tell him I believe he can become a great knight if he learns to shut his mouth."

Then, Sergeant Bertrand closed his eyes. William felt a need to say something, but didn't really know what. Finally, he said, "Thank you, Sergeant. I am grateful for your advice."

William went back to the stables and helped Louis finish loading the wagon, saddling his horse, and securing the other horses to the back of the wagon. Then, they departed. They rode without talking at a slow pace through town in the dark of night. They felt like thieves escaping a crime. Leaving Sergeant Bertrand behind was tough, even though they knew they had no real choice. After leaving the town, they continued west at a slow pace due to the darkness until about two hours before sunrise. William stopped and said, "Let's give the horses a little rest until the sun comes up. We should both eat something, too."

Chapter 30

About a week later, Henry was brought before the Cardinal
for a second time. After his first meeting with the Cardinal, he and
Garrard were taken to separate cells. Henry was given fresh water to
clean himself and a blanket to cover himself with at night. Also, the
frequency and quality of his food increased. Only he and the
Cardinal were in the room at this second meeting.

Without preamble, the Cardinal said, "Do you know anything
about a creature known as Baphomet?"

Henry was taken aback and not sure how to respond. After a
short pause, he replied, "I apologize, Your Eminence, but did you
say Mohomet?"

"No. I said Baphomet, and don't play games. If you know
anything, you need to tell me now!" the Cardinal said.

Without hesitation, Henry said, "I don't know what that is.
I've never heard of it."

Visibly relaxing, the Cardinal said, "I didn't think you did.
Sir Henry, I have come to believe that you may be innocent. But I'm
afraid most of your brothers in the Templar Order are a different
story. The Inquisition discovered that the heart of blackness that
resides in the Knights Templar is a demon named Baphomet; most
of your fellow knights were, and are still, willing servants of this
foul beast from Hell. As a matter of fact, Henry, there are very few
of the knights among your Order who have not already confessed to
worshipping this creature, including your Grand Master. Yet there
are a few, like yourself, who have not. I am inclined to believe that
you may have been unaware of what was happening. It's possible
you would have been indoctrinated into this unholy doctrine at a
later date, but at this time, I believe that you are ignorant of any of
this. I am inclined to release you and possibly allow you to join the
Knight Hospitaller or take Holy Orders with another group of monks
if you so desire."

Henry was stunned. His first thought was to deny what the
Cardinal said about his fellow knights. He wanted to point out that
they probably only confessed due to torture, but he knew that would
fall on deaf ears and only worsen his situation. Besides, Henry
didn't want the opportunity of getting released to be taken away due

to his own stubbornness. Perhaps once he was released, he could find a way to help his brothers.

The Cardinal waited patiently while all this ran through Henry's head. Finally, the Cardinal said impatiently, "Sir Henry, although I didn't exactly ask you a question, I believe some type of response is in order."

Henry cleared his throat and said, "I'm sorry, Your Eminence, but the last few weeks have struck me to the core. Everything I have lived for, and the Rule I have lived by, has been shattered. It is difficult for me to accept all that has happened. Yet I know the Church is a Holy and trustworthy institution. I still believe in and am committed to the pledges I made upon joining the Templars, but it appears that the organization no longer exists and may have never been what I believed it to be. If you allow me, I would be glad to join the Knights Hospitaller. Their Rule is similar to the one I have already been living by. Perhaps I can redeem myself for having blindly believed in the organization I was a part of.

The Cardinal said in as kindly a tone as he could muster, "Do not be overly hard on yourself, my son. Evil is deceitful and cunning. I believe that the Templars' origins and much of their history demonstrate that they were once a true and powerful force, committed to God and His Holy Church. Sadly, it appears one of your leaders at some time in the past was beguiled by this creature from Hell, and it has brought the destruction of this once great instrument of God. The Church will redeem the souls of those willing to accept forgiveness and cleanse the world of those who are unrepentant. As for you, Sir Henry, I have anticipated that you would accept my offer to join the Hospitallers. I have taken the liberty to speak to the head of the local commandery, and he has agreed to take you and six other men of the Temple into the Order on a probationary basis. If you prove yourself loyal to God, the Church, and the Hospitallers, perhaps they will accept you as a full brother. At some point, you may even be made a brother knight."

"I won't be a knight when I become a Hospitaller?" Henry asked, somewhat confused.

"No. You will be entering the organization as a novice monk. You will need to spend at least a year in prayer and service before being considered for admission as a brother of the

Hospitallers. After that, you can petition to take vows to become a knight again. If you decide to follow this path, you will be stripped of the privileges and responsibilities of being a knight. You will no longer be a member of the chivalry until such time as the Hospitallers deem it appropriate, if ever."

Henry felt his face redden as anger began to well up in him. But he forced himself to calm down, "I will accept this offer in the hope that I am found worthy to once again serve as a knight." It may have been the hardest thing Henry had ever said in his life, but he felt he must. He must get out from under the control of men sent by the King and the Church to destroy the Templars and all that they stood for. Henry decided it would be best to bide his time and wait until he was fully trusted before attempting to clear the Templar name. Although he previously may have had a few doubts about the Templars, he knew at that moment that no evil, sinister demon was pervading the Order. The only evil was that these men were trying to convince themselves that they were doing good by dismantling the Order for their own nefarious reasons. In the end, they would pay. He would see to that.

Chapter 31

Although Derrick had traveled more than most commoners, he still had little concept of how far it would be to take Mary to Rennes-le-Chateau. Derrick also didn't quite know how to begin a journey that would cover such a distance. He didn't like the idea of traveling by road. Derrick was much more comfortable sticking to the forests, where they could avoid other people, but that would make the long walk even longer and their movement much slower. When he questioned Mary about where Rennes-le-Château was or how to get there, he soon realized that her meager experience of traveling in France far outweighed his own.

They began by gathering all their provisions. They had more dried meat than Darrick felt they should carry. Darrick gathered a few dried herbs and ointments used for medical purposes, some of which he also used in stews. As they were rolling the items they would take with them into tanned hides that could also be unrolled and used as shelter from the weather, Mary asked, "Do you have any money?"

Darrick said, "Yes, some, I'll get it." He retreated into his dwelling, and when he returned, he was carrying a good-sized leather pouch. "This is all I have. Sometimes, people from the city want some of my smoked venison or the skins I trade with, but don't have anything I want, so I trade for money. I usually don't have any reason to use it to buy items that I can easily trade for, so it just sits around. Forgot all about it, to be honest."

Mary opened the pouch and looked inside. Her eyes widened, and she looked back at Darrick, open-mouthed. Darrick, unsure what was upsetting her, said, "I'm sorry. That's all I have."

Mary threw her arms around Darrick's neck and hugged him tightly. Darrick froze. He couldn't move. He liked the sensation of her being close to him, but was also extremely uncomfortable, nearly to the point of panic. Mary soon released her grip when she realized how rigid Darrick had become. She dropped her arms, took half a step back, and said, "By most people's standards, Darrick, you would be considered rich with all this money. Most common people don't make this much money in a year's time."

Still somewhat uncomfortable, Darrick finally said, "Well, I don't understand its value. You carry it and use it as you see fit."

Mary replied, "No. We should each put some in our packs and keep some hidden inside our clothes. Do you have a smaller bag where we can put just a few coins? We must keep all the rest hidden and packed in such a way that it won't make noise. We need to appear poor and of no importance so that we will not attract attention."

Darrick said, "I have one small bag and lots of light leather we can use to make more bags or pouches to put the rest of the coins in, but what about you?"

Mary looked confused. "What about me?"

Darrick cleared his throat and said, "Well, even with us dressed as poor folk not worth robbing, we will still draw attention. You are too pretty to go unnoticed, and, as you've already experienced, some men may try to force themselves on you. I will attempt to protect you, but although I'm good with a bow and forest craft, I'm no warrior. I would die to protect you, but that won't save your honor or get you any closer to your goal."

Mary was silent for a moment, gaping at Darrick. Then she stepped toward Darrick and quickly kissed him on the cheek: "You are possibly the nicest and wisest man I have ever met."

This was the second time in his life that he could recall being kissed on the cheek. He felt the same rush of feelings: desire, warmth, bewilderment, happiness. But this time, he felt caution and fear. It had taken him some time to get over Francia. Her memory had haunted his dreams for some time. He didn't want to experience that again.

Mary said, "Get me two pieces of that thin leather, maybe one foot by five feet and another two feet by five feet. And I'll need some of that cord you have, a knife, and your awl. I also need one of your shirts and a pair of your breeches to wear."

They spent the rest of the day with Darrick making pouches that were sewn into their traveling clothes and the leather they used to roll their belongings in. Meanwhile, Mary worked on her two leather projects but refused to tell Darrick what she was doing. In the late afternoon, Darrick finished making the pouches and started cooking dinner when Mary announced, "I believe this will do." She stood up, stretched, and asked Darrick for his good skinning knife. After he handed it to her, she gathered the two leather pieces she had been working on, the pants and shirt Darrick had retrieved for her, and some of the clothes and coins they had divided for her to carry. She told Darrick, "Stay here. I'm just going behind some of those trees."

Darrick continued to prepare the meal. After about twenty minutes, Mary returned, but she no longer looked like Mary. She no longer looked entirely like a woman if you ignored the feminine features of her face. Her breasts seemed to have disappeared, she looked to have gained substantial weight around her middle, and, most disorienting, her hair had been roughly cut off. Darrick stared at her for some time. Mary turned in a complete circle. "What do you think?" she asked.

Darrick said in a shocked voice, "What did you do?"

Mary, with a laugh, said, "I used one piece of the leather to bind my breasts so that they are not so prominent. I sewed the other leather into a large pouch, which I filled with some of my clothes and the coins; I tied it around my middle to make me look fat. Then, by wearing your clothes and cutting my hair off, I completed the transformation into a man."

Darrick looked at her critically and then walked to the cookfire. He took some of the ash and dirt, rubbing them together in his hands as he walked toward Mary. Darrick said, "Your face is still too pretty. May I?" he held out his dirty hands.

Mary smiled and said, "Please."

Darrick began to rub the dirt and soot on her face and neck. After he finished, he stepped back and looked at her again. He said thoughtfully, "Perhaps... if they don't look too closely."

Mary said, "It'll work, but you'll have to do all the talking. If people ask, you can tell them I'm a mute."

Darrick said, "Ok, we leave tomorrow morning. Let's eat now and get a good night's rest. We have a long walk ahead of us."

143

Chapter 32

The men of the Holy Inquisition were used to others being terrified around them, but this was different. The man was not afraid of them. As a matter of fact, he seemed to find some perverse feeling of safety in their presence. This somewhat unsettled the monks. When the man was first brought before them, they assumed he was mad. Later, they began to suspect he was also possessed, but when they gave him a cross, he kissed it and refused to give it back. They had two guards try to force it from him, but they stopped when they realized he would rather die than release his hold on it. They soon understood that the crucifix had a calming effect on Odo, and he was more likely to answer their questions intelligibly while holding it. As they questioned him further, some began to believe that here was finally the truth about the corruption that pervaded the Knights Templar. They thought that this creature of hell, Baphomet, was clearly not a creation of this squire, Odo. They didn't think any simple man could create this evil being out of their imagination. Obviously, he was terrified of Baphomet. Baphomet was plainly a construct of Hell, and somehow, Odo had survived his interaction with the demon and maintained his mortal soul. The confrontation with Baphomet had driven Odo slightly mad. However, he was still a useful tool to them if they could only obtain more information from Odo.

It became apparent that they needed help in calming and directing Odo so that he would stop babbling. They asked Odo if there was someone he knew and trusted who could be brought in to help them understand more about this creature and its control over the Templars. Odo said there was a Father Falardeau that he trusted. When they looked for this man, it was discovered that when they attempted to arrest him, he had died due to the stress. Odo then mentioned Father Thomas. The Inquisition discovered he was at the Paris commandry, and they quickly sent for him.

Father Thomas was brought before three Inquisitors, one of whom was Brother Jaye, who said, "As I explained to you earlier, we need your help in speaking to Odo regarding Baphomet. Upon discovering the truth about the organization he once served, he has become somewhat hysterical. We need to determine what Odo knows about Baphomet, including whether there is an idol that the

Templars venerate, if it ever appears to them in a physical form, and if it has any other names. Most importantly, we need to know if Odo knows anything about the forms of worship this creature requires of the Templars."

Thomas replied with his head bowed, "I will find out what I can. Am I to be taken to him now?"

Brother Jaye said, "No, you will question him here, before us. Although it appears you are willingly helping us against your former Order, we still have some reservations regarding your loyalty."

Thomas looked up at them and said in a less than meek voice, "Guillaume de Nogaret recruited me to discover the Templars' secrets by becoming a trusted advisor. I have done nothing that was not in the service of the Crown of France and the Holy Church. I do not understand why my loyalties are still in question."

In his quiet, calm voice, Brother Jaye replied, "When you became a brother of the Templars, did you not take their vows?"

"Yes, but it was only…" was all Thomas got out before the quiet voice interrupted him.

"And those vows were sworn before the cross and under the consecration of God, yet you claim all the while you were working against the organization. So, either you made vows before God that were lies, or you are lying to us now. Either way, we must establish who you are truly loyal to. But that is enough of that. Let us get on with the issue we brought you here for. Guards, please bring Odo in."

When Odo was brought in, nearly dragged by two guards, Thomas barely recognized him. The last time Thomas saw Odo, he was a healthy-looking lad of perhaps seventeen years old. Now, Odo had the appearance of a man more than twice that age. He was filthy and dressed in rags, putting off quite an offensive odor. Previously, Odo had been a quiet and, to Thomas, an intelligent and introspective individual; this man, however, was clearly unhinged and couldn't stop muttering to himself. Thomas wasn't even confident that Odo knew where he was, as he just knelt there, where the guards released him, clutching a crucifix and occasionally kissing it.

After the guards left the room and closed the door, Brother Jaye said in his smooth, low voice, "Odo, we have brought Father Thomas as you requested."

Odo suddenly looked up straight at Thomas, and Thomas plainly saw the insanity that resided in those eyes. He wondered what use he could possibly be in questioning someone whose world was so completely removed from reality. Odo crawled to where Thomas was, wrapped his arms around Thomas' legs, and began to weep, saying softly, "Thank the Virgin."

Not used to comforting people, Thomas hesitantly reached out and patted Odo on the head and said, "It'll be alright, my son."

Brother Jaye let this continue for a few moments, perhaps enjoying the discomfort displayed in every aspect of Thomas. Then, he said, "Odo, we have brought a chair for you to sit in so that you can tell Father Thomas what you know about Baphomet. He has come here to be of service to you so that we might attempt to rescue as many of the lost souls among the Knights Templar."

Odo looked up and visibly tried to calm himself. For a brief instant, Thomas saw the old Odo. Then the eyes darted from left to right, and the look of terror and insanity overtook him again. Odo came to his feet, went to the chair, and sat down. Brother Jaye said, "We have told Father Thomas what you have revealed to us about this foul creature, but we would like you to tell the good Father in your own words."

Odo looked from Brother Jaye to Thomas and asked Thomas, "You'll stay with me and protect me, won't you, Father Thomas?"

Before Thomas could think of what to say, Brother Jaye answered for him, "The good Father is here at your disposal, Odo. He will stay with you until we can banish this demon back to Hell, and you no longer have to worry about it."

Odo seemed relieved and looked up at Thomas, who was standing a few feet in front of him. He said, "Thank you. Where would you like me to start?"

Brother Jay said, "Start when you first heard of this creature and how you came to know of its working within the Templars."

Odo sat up a little in his chair, gripped the crucifix more tightly, and began, "I first heard about Baphomet a few years ago. It was from some of the older knights who had been to Outremer. They were talking amongst themselves, and I don't believe they noticed that I was listening. I wasn't being sneaky or anything; I was going about my business while they talked. At first, I thought they were talking about the Muslim prophet Muhammad. As I continued to listen, I heard them very clearly say, "Baphomet." They sometimes referred to Baphomet as an individual creature, and at other times, it seemed as if they were referring to Baphomet as a group of people. At the time, I assumed that this Baphomet was either an idol worshiped by the infidels or a group of people whom they had fought in the Holy Lands. I really didn't think about it much after that. Maybe if I had, I could have done something to stop its spread." Odo then fell to his knees and said, "God, please forgive me. I did not know."

Brother Jaye said, "God understands that you did not truly understand what you heard, and He forgives you. Now, please sit back down and continue."

Odo looked at Father Jaye and then at Thomas as if asking his opinion. Thomas indicated the chair to Odo to show he agreed with Father Jaye. Odo resumed his seat and continued, "It wasn't until I was locked in the commandery that God revealed the truth to me. I heard two others who were also locked up with me talking in low tones about how Baphomet would free them. They must have noticed that I heard them, because that night, in my dreams, I was attacked by a creature. I knew instantly that the beast was Baphomet, and I saw that he was going to kill me because God had shown me the truth.

"Baphomet was just about to reach out and crush my soul when I was jerked awake by the hand of God. I was instantly aware of the truth. I knew that if God hadn't woken me, Baphomet would have killed me in my sleep. I also knew that Baphomet was a demon; he was the cause of the loss of the Holy Lands and the corruption of the Knights Templar. God told me that this creature had beguiled the leaders of the Templars while they were in Outremer. Upon their return, they had brought this spawn of Hell with them. The Templar command had slowly indoctrinated other knights in the Order to forsake Christ and begin to worship Baphomet.

"God showed me that they did this during the secret meetings they held in the dark of night. That is why only knights were allowed to attend those meetings and why they left a knight with his

147

sword drawn guarding the meeting room. That is also why the knights were never allowed to say what they had discussed. Once they had all the knights converted to this vile creature, the Templars would begin converting the rest of Christendom to their unholy worship. If anyone opposed them, they would just put them to the sword.

"So many things make sense now. This is the reason for our abandonment of the Holy Lands. It is why the Templars still maintained so large a standing army even with no one left to fight and why everything is so secretive."

Father Thomas was stunned by all that Odo had said and how clearly he explained things. Perhaps the lad was not insane; maybe he was touched by God, and the experience had unnerved him. All of Thomas's attention was focused on Odo; he even forgot about the Brothers of the Inquisition seated near him. He noticed that blood was dripping from Odo's hands as he gripped the crucifix fiercely.

Thomas, still standing, knelt to one knee before Odo and asked, "You said you saw this Baphomet in a dream. What did it look like?"

Odo got a far-away look in his eyes and said in a quiet voice, "It stood upright like a man, but it had the head and legs of a goat with long curled horns. It was covered in hair from the neck up and the knees down. The rest of it was completely naked. It spoke to me in another language; I couldn't understand what it said, but I knew that it was evil. I wish I knew what it said, and at the same time, I am glad I don't. The voice was deep and harsh. It seemed to be laughing while it spoke to me."

Thomas asked, "Do you recall any of the words it said or at least what they sounded like?"

Odo's face grew tense in concentration, and he said, "I think one word sounded like 'perdere,' another like 'orbis terrarium,' and another like 'templum' and 'anima mea.' I don't recall any others."

One of the Brothers of the Inquisition drew in a breath sharply and broke Thomas and Odo's trance. Thomas, now feeling a kinship with the young Odo who was apparently suffering from the weight God had placed on him, put a hand on Odo's and said, "Relax your grip on the crucifix, my son. You have done well and aided us so that we can defeat the demon through the Power of Christ and compel it back to Hell."

Brother Jaye then added, "Father Thomas is correct, my son. If you return to your room, we will converse with Father Thomas."

Odo, who had visibly relaxed after Thomas spoke to him, suddenly tensed and cried out as if in pain, "No! You said the father would stay with me. I need his protection. Otherwise, Baphomet will consume my soul."

Thomas squeezed Odo's hand slightly, drawing his attention back to him. While looking at Odo, he said to Brother Jaye, "Perhaps Odo can wait outside the door with the guards while we talk. Afterward, I will go with him to the chapel, where we can pray."

Brother Jaye, who was not used to people making suggestions to him, looked slightly annoyed but quickly calmed himself before he spoke: "Perhaps that would be best." Then, Brother Jaye added to Odo, "Do not worry, my son, no evil will befall you here. We consecrated these grounds before we started our examinations into these dark matters."

Odo, still not entirely convinced, was mollified and went with the guards, whom Brother Jaye had called back into the chamber. Brother Jaye looked at Thomas and said, "It appears you are not useless to us after all. Odo has disclosed more to you in one meeting than we have gotten in hours of questioning."

One of the other Brothers spoke for the first time, saying, "The words he recalled: 'world,' 'destroy,' 'temple,' and 'soul.' These seem to be a clear indication of dark manifestations within the Templars and evil plots to destroy the Church."

The third Brother added in a voice filled with contempt, "I still believe the lad is insane or making all this up just to get better treatment. You can't possibly believe this. He describes a creature that all Christendom would readily identify as a demon. I've heard priests describe the Devil himself in just such a way. Do you truly believe someone who spent years in a monastic Order like the Templars wouldn't recognize Latin? How many Latin Masses do you suppose he's attended? He knows the meaning of those words as well as any of us."

Thomas then spoke, "I don't deny that the description he offered for Baphomet is common knowledge, but have you considered it a classic description for a reason? Might it not be that the accounts we have all heard were given to us so we would know evil when it came before us? And as for the Latin words he recalled,

149

although I have not known him for long, I know this much about Odo: he has very little guile in him. You are correct that he has attended many Masses, and the squires do receive some training in Latin, but they are by no means fluent. I agree he should have recognized it as Latin. Still, perhaps the demon did not want him to understand what was being said, so it confounded Odo's mind. Possibly, it is only by the Grace of God that he has recalled those few words."

This did not seem to pacify the contemptuous Brother. Before anyone could speak further, Brother Jaye said, "I see we have more digging to do before we can root out this evil. I want answers about this Baphomet. I want to know the truth before we ask further questions about the Templar leadership. That way, we know who to press until we get the answers we know to be true. Let us not forget, Brothers, we are here to do God's work, find the truth, and force the men to admit to their complicity in this evil business so we can save their souls, even if we must destroy their bodies."

Chapter 33

Several men of Clermont had been drinking at the bar, trying to talk each other into taking matters into their own hands and arresting or hanging the Templars among them; it depended on who was talking loudest at the time. They had become certain that the men in the stable were Templars hiding here, intending to spread their vile perversions in Clermont. The men in the bar damn well were not going to let that happen. Several times, they almost made it to the door leading out of the bar when someone would bring up some flaw in their plan or question their certainty that these men were indeed Templars, or want them to wait for someone to finish his drink or take a piss or something. It wasn't until the barkeeper told them he was closing, and they had to leave, that they decided to "Do something about those damned Templars."

The fifteen or so tramped off to the stables behind the bar: one fell face down and passed out, and the others didn't really notice. It took three of them five minutes to open the barn door. It took another ten minutes for them to agree that the men, wagon, mules, and horses were not hiding somewhere in the twenty-by-thirty-foot building. They had just about decided to head home when someone recalled that one of those evil Templars was sick and being cared for by Michael. So, once they found the barn door again, they stumbled around to the back where Michael's shack was. They pounded on the door until Michael opened it and then pushed their way inside, shouting incoherently about "Templars" and "heretics" and "hang 'em." Michael waited patiently for them to quiet, which finally happened shortly after the loudest of their group vomited in a corner.

Michael said in a clear but angry voice, "You men had better go home. There are no Templars or heretics here."

One of the men in the mob slurred, "We knows you beens healing one of them. Where's he at?"

Michael replied, "There was a man here whom I was trying to help, but if he was a Templar, that's news to me. But even if he were one, it'd do you no good to hang him. He lies right there dead. So, unless you want to help me bury him, I suggest you leave."

Not yet mollified but braver upon realizing there would be no fight with trained warriors, three of them went to the body lying on a pallet to have a closer look. After examining the body, the three declared that the man was indeed dead and left Michael's shack to go to their various homes.

Shortly after William and Louis left Clermont, Michael went for Father Patrick at Sergeant Bertrand's request. Michael waited outside the shack as the Priest gave Bertrand the Last Rites. Well over an hour later, Father Patrick told Michael to come in. The Priest and Michael talked quietly as the Sergeant's labored breathing grew slower and more hesitant.

Father Patrick asked, "Did you know this man well?"

"No," replied Michael. "Two young men brought him to me a few days ago. The wound had already turned bad by the time he arrived. I did what I could, but it was beyond my skill."

The Father said in the same tone, "Did you know he was a Templar?"

Michael paused a moment, then quietly answered, "Yes. Do you believe what they are saying about them?"

Father Patrick nearly chuckled and said, "No. I've known many Templar clergy and even been acquainted with a few knights. Some are overly proud for my taste, but they were all good men; after listening to this man's confession, I can honestly say I've never met a more honorable man, especially considering all the death and destruction he witnessed. I can't tell you what he said to me, but he carried great guilt for many things that were not wrong in the eyes of the Church or God. Even though he was aware that the Church approved of his actions, he felt grievous guilt for some of them."

Michael said, "Men who fight in war, even a war sanctioned by the Church, carry great guilt that those who were not there cannot understand. Killing an enemy, especially after you've seen friends killed, may be easy for most of us. But when all is quiet, and the anger, fear, and excitement have burned out, you feel spent and shaky. And then you start to think too much. At that point, you have a choice: shove those thoughts and feelings aside for a later time when you are not at war, sear your conscience, and become a killing machine with no sympathy, or quit. After six or seven months, I quit fighting and started learning to care for the wounded. I spent two more years in the Holy Lands, but I never carried a weapon again."

The Father asked, "You felt excitement in battle?"

152

Michael replied, "Yes. Most of us would say it was the dominant feeling during battle. There's fear that you might die at any moment, but even that causes a type of excitement. Everything becomes more distinct, things seem to happen slowly, and you notice more detail; it's odd. Afterward, you're so excited you're alive and uninjured; it's the greatest feeling in the world. I think that sensation is why some men are drawn to warfare. The closest thing I can compare it to is how I feel after a terrible storm has passed. Do you recall the storm we had three years ago that tore the roofs off many buildings, and the lightning crashed with an awful loud booming sound? During the strong winds, booming, and crashing, you couldn't imagine anything outside surviving. Then, the storm almost instantly blew out, and it was bright and sunny. The entire town came out to assess the damage and assist one another. Those who had no real damage were overjoyed and willing to help others who had not made it through unscathed. People who were previously at odds with each other over petty squabbles did whatever they could for their former adversaries; they brought food, helped repair roofs, whatever. That is maybe just a sliver of what it's like after a battle.

"Those Templars, Hospitallers, and other knights dedicated to staying and holding the Holy Lands couldn't quit fighting as I chose to do. They fought for years. Because Europe lost interest and stopped sending troops to help, we have decided to blame those warrior monks, despite the fact that they did not have the necessary resources. I have nothing but respect for the Templars. I will never believe what that popinjay King of ours says or even the puppet Pope he has as his prisoner in Avignon."

Father Patrick looked at Michael with a sidelong glance and said, "I agree with you about the Templars, but I would watch who is around when you make comments about the King like that. Although I agree the situation with Pope Clement V is somewhat troubling, I would remind you that he is still the Church's head. I expect you in confession this week for that comment."

Michael chuckled and said contritely, "Yes, Father." After a pause, he added, "I believe the good Sergeant has passed on and is finally at peace."

The Father said, "I will see that he is buried in the church graveyard. Let us pray."

Chapter 34

William and Louis continued east. On the second day, it began to rain, a cold, bone-chilling rain. The rain was unrelenting and lasted for days. They plodded on, passing through a small hamlet and town. The road grew so muddy that they spent more and more time getting the wagon out of the muck it was continually getting stuck in. William called a halt when they reached a spot with enough open area off the roadway to park the wagon. Louis went into the woods to find some firewood that wasn't thoroughly soaked, but almost immediately returned.

He was a little out of breath but called out to be heard above the rain, "Sir William, there's a cave here just through those trees. I think, with a little clearing, we can get the wagon through to it. It looks plenty big enough for us, the horses, mules, and the wagon."

William said, "You stay here and watch the wagon. Get me a dry piece of cloth I can use for a torch, and I'll get some oil and the flint and steel. Hopefully, no wild animal has already taken up residence in it."

William then put the cloth under his leather gambeson, found a good three-foot branch, and entered the mouth of the cave. He wrapped the mostly dry material around the end of the branch and poured the oil over the fabric. He struck flint to steel a few times until he got a good spark to ignite the oil. William found himself standing in a large cave: the mouth was undoubtedly large enough to accommodate them all. He yelled to Louis, "Start clearing a path for the wagon. I'm going to see how far back the cave goes and make sure there are no large animals to worry about."

He drew his sword and began to head deeper into the cave. The cave extended quite a way back. The walls were several feet apart, so he stayed in the middle, steadily moving the torch to both sides so that he could keep track of the walls and any shafts that might travel off the main cave. The cave's ceiling was high enough that he could easily walk upright without worrying about hitting his head. He feared that at any moment, the flickering light from the torch would reveal the standing form of a bear: mouth dripping with saliva, snarling, with arms and claws outstretched to shred him to pieces. The bear he did encounter was not what he had been fearing.

He had gone back at least 100 feet from the entrance before he noticed any narrowing of the cave. The cave wall turned to the left, and as he came closer, he saw for the first time that there were figures on the wall. The bear he faced was painted on the cave, and there were figures of men with spears attacking the bear. As he looked around more, he noticed paintings all over the walls. By his torchlight, he could see that the paintings were mostly colored in red, yellow, and black. Some creatures he recognized. There were humans, horses, stags, cows, and bulls. But there were also paintings of symbols that he could not put a meaning to, and creatures that seemed to be imaginary. At first, he thought the images were the workings of children. Then, as he looked more closely, he became aware that there was something beautiful about the illustrations. Their simplicity seemed to tell a story, a complex one of life, struggle, and death. Everywhere he looked, he saw more paintings. There were even paintings on the ceiling. After several minutes, he recalled what he was supposed to be doing and remembered Louis and the wagon.

He went a little deeper into the cave and saw no fresh signs of animals, so he decided he had gone far enough. He returned to the mouth of the cave just in time to hear Louis complain, "Louis, go clear a path in the pouring rain while I go into the nice dry cave and wait for you. I'm sure as soon as we get the wagon and horses in the cave, I'll be sent back out into the rain to try and find something resembling dry firewood."

William suddenly appeared out of the rain next to Louis. He decided to ignore Louis' comments as just the complaining common to all underlings. William said, "Looks like you've cleared enough to get the wagon through here. Let's move it and the animals into the cave, and then I'll go look for dry firewood."

Louis opened his mouth to say something, but the correct response didn't come to him. William looked at him and said, "Close your mouth, or you'll drown. I think it's raining harder."

About two hours later, the horses and mules were brushed and as dry as they could get them. The wagon was parked in the cave, and they had two fires burning: one near the entrance and one a little further back, closer to the animals. They had a good supply of wood drying near the two fires. While getting the wood, William had flushed a rabbit out of a thicket; he killed it by kicking it as it tried to run past him. The rabbit was now being roasted.

After they had eaten, William showed Louis the wall paintings. Louis was entranced by them and asked, "Who do you think painted these? Some of these creatures can't be real, like this stag; those antlers are larger than the animal. I get the feeling these pictures are here to tell us something. They must be several hundred years old. The only weapons I see are spears and rocks. They don't even have bows. In some of the stories of the battles between the Jews and Canaanites, they have better weapons than this."

William said, "I don't know who painted these, but I'm sure they are older than a few hundred years. Those stories of the battles between the Jews and the Canaanites are from over a thousand years ago. I think these are much older."

Louis asked, "How old is the world? I always thought God created the Earth a couple of thousand years ago. Who do you think the people were that painted these?"

William said, "You're asking the wrong person."

Louis said, "Looking at these makes me wonder about a lot of things. The priests and the Commanders, you Knights, and... well... just about everyone tells me 'This is how it is' and 'that is the truth,' but how does anyone know? I'm told to love my neighbor as I love myself, but to kill the infidel because he has different beliefs. That doesn't make sense to me. Do you think the Priests even know about these paintings? I don't see any crosses or other recognizable religious symbols. So, were these people not religious, did they not want to paint their religion, or are the animals their religion? Although it seems funny that they'd kill the animals if that were their God... although I guess we killed ours...I'm very confused."

William looked at Louis with new respect and said, "You've thought about this way more than I have. I didn't know you contemplated things so profoundly, Louis. I believed you just talked and never even considered what you were saying.

Louis said, "I talk so much in an attempt to drown out all these questions I have. It doesn't work very well, but it's better than letting my brain spin free." After a pause, Louis said, "I do have another question that I hope you can answer. What are we going to do now? We started with two knights, a Sergeant-at-arms, a priest, and two squires, and we're down to just the two of us. It seems like this trip has been doomed from the start. Do you think we can protect the wagon if some brigands try to take it? No offense. I know you're a trained knight, and I have been training for years to become a knight, but Sergeant Bertrand... well... he was scary in a fight; he killed men before I even knew the fight had started."

William had thought along these same lines already and replied, "I know things haven't gone as planned, but we still must complete our mission. As miserable as this rain has been, I believe it's kept anyone from following us. I think if we turn onto the first road heading south, we should begin the last leg of the journey. It was hard to lose Sergeant Bertrand, especially how we abandoned him... I hated leaving him, but we were forced to. We must get this wagon and its contents to their destination. We have orders that clearly outline what we need to do to continue, regardless of the cost. We must complete this mission."

Louis said, "Maybe after we get rid of this wagon, we can head back to Clermont; perhaps the Sergeant's still alive."

William shook his head, "I don't think he has survived. You didn't see him before we left. He looked gray and nearly dead already. I could smell his wound from outside the door to the shack. If he survived, it'd be a true miracle. Besides, I don't think we should return that way. After we leave Rennes-le-Château, we should head east to the coast and then make our way to Avignon to seek an audience with the Pope or, at the very least, a Cardinal. Maybe we can get answers to our questions regarding these arrests. Maybe you'll get a chance to ask about these cave paintings."

Two days later, the rain stopped. William and Louis decided to go hunting and gathering to replenish their supplies. At the same time, they gave the roads time to dry. They snared a rabbit and found some wild grapes and some wild onions that were mostly still good. That night, they made stew with rabbit and onions. The next morning, anxious to get going, they started off.

The next several days were enjoyable: the weather was nearly summer-like, and although there was a cold bite in the air at night, the days were perfect for riding. One early morning, they entered the town of Toulouse. They had decided it was unsafe to linger in Toulouse to wait for their friends, who had returned to Paris, as planned. Yet, William and Louis agreed to stop just long enough to check to see if the others were there. William stopped at the first pub they came across, as they had all agreed to do when they divided up. He went in hoping to see Henry, Odo, and possibly even Thomas or Mary, but it was a vain wish. He bought some food and supplies, and they set off on their way before noon without attracting any undue attention.

As they began to draw near Rennes-le-Chateau, William grew nervous. What if the Templars and, particularly, Father Lull, whom he was supposed to meet, had been arrested? What if there was no one there? Was he supposed to return to Paris with the crate? He figured they were only a few hours from their goal. He was just about to call a halt so he could ride ahead alone and scout out the area when he saw a sight on a hill that startled him and almost made him weep.

There was a massive warhorse covered in a white and black caparison with large red crosses on the side, and on the horse's back sat a knight holding a lance. The knight's head was helmetless, but he wore a chain mail coif. A white surcoat with a red cross pattee on his chest covered most of the chain mail that protected his body. The knight sat motionless, looking down on them: a silent sentinel cloaked in honor and bravery. William suddenly felt ashamed for not wearing his Templar surcoat.

William told Louis, "Wait here while I go treat with this Templar." He then rode off up the hill.

Louis said to himself, "Wait here. Do this. Carry that. Just once, I'd like to hear, 'Louis, what do you think we should do?'"

William rode up to within twenty feet of the Templar and raised his right hand, showing it was empty. "I am Sir William de Sevrey, Knight Templar of the Paris Commandry. I was sent here by the Grand Master Jacques de Molay. I am supposed to meet with Father Lull to deliver the crate on the wagon." He chose not to mention the letter he also carried.

The other knight looked William up and down, then thrust the spike on the butt end of his lance into the ground. Raising his now empty right hand, he said, "I am Sir Frances de Charentes, presently of Rennes-le-Chateau. It appears the order of dress for a Knight of the Temple has changed since I was last in Paris.

William, somewhat put off by the arrogance in the man's tone, said, "That, Sir, is a long story that I'd rather tell after I have completed the Grand Master's business."

158

Sir Frances said, "Very well. Follow me if you will." He retrieved his lance, turned his destrier around, and rode down the back side of the hill.

William turned in his saddle, whistled, and waved for Louis to follow, and then rode off to keep in sight of the knight.

Louis snapped the reins to get the mules moving and spoke again to himself, "Now I don't even get words to tell me to do something. I get a whistle like I'm a dog and a hand gesture. I can do hand gestures, too."

After perhaps thirty minutes, the town of Rennes-le-Chateau came into sight. They eventually arrived at the church, where Sir Frances dismounted and waited for William and Louis to catch up. As William got off his horse, a bald, slightly overweight priest with an easy smile came out of the church. The priest, who was perhaps fifty years old, said to Sir Frances, "Ah, Sir Frances, I see you've brought us a couple of guests. I can tell by your demeanor that these gentlemen must be dear friends of yours."

"This knight claims to be a Templar sent by Grand Master Jacques de Moley to see you, Father Lull. So now that I have delivered him, I will return to my watch," Sir Frances said as his scowl deepened.

Father Lull, with an amused look on his face, said with a wink to Louis, "I am deeply indebted, Sir Frances, and look forward to our next meeting with great enthusiasm." As Sir Frances rode away, Father Lull added to both William and Louis, "I shouldn't irritate Sir Frances so much, but it is so difficult not to. The man has two facial expressions, disappointment and irritation, which are almost identical. Yet I have taken a holy vow to make him smile just once before I die."

Before William could think of anything to say, Louis replied, "From the little contact I have had with Sir Frances, I think you might want to amend that holy vow to making him smile when you die."

William was taken aback that even Louis would make such a comment and said, "I am sorry, Father. My squire is often very..." but broke off due to the gales of laughter that suddenly burst from Father Lull.

It was some time before the father could regain his composure and control his laughter. He said to William, "No apology is needed. I can tell this squire is a man after my own heart. I hold a record at Clairvaux Abbey for the number of times I was almost rejected as a candidate for the priesthood due to speaking inappropriate, yet usually true, statements. However, let us proceed with the business at hand before we stray any further off track. As Sir Frances said, I am Father Lull. And you two are?"

William said, "I am Sir William de Sevrey, and although I may not be attired as such, I am a Knight of the Temple from the Paris Commandry. This young man is Louis, my squire."

Father Lull said, "Why has the Grand Master sent you here, and how did you escape Paris? We have heard that all the knights were arrested along with most of the other members of the Order."

William looked to Louis and then back at the father, "Well, you seem better informed than we are. Perhaps you and I should speak inside while Louis waits here to watch the wagon."

Father Lull grinned his infectious smile and said, "There's no need for Louis to wait out here. The wagon and its contents are perfectly safe, as are you. Although it is a beautiful day out, I'm sure Louis would like a glass of wine and some food while we talk. Come along." With that, Father Lull turned and walked up the steps to the round church.

William and Louis followed the Father through the church and soon found themselves in a small rectory. Father Lull had poured a glass of wine for all three of them and set out a plate with bread, cheese, and grapes.

The good Father said, "Now, why did the Grand Master send you two?"

William took out the sealed envelope and handed it to the father. "The Grand Master told me to give this to you. I'm sorry to question your judgment, Father, but I am uncomfortable leaving the wagon unattended. I would feel better if Louis watched the wagon and its contents while we talked."

"Nonsense. I'll send Jon, my acolyte, to move the wagon into the stables, where it will be perfectly safe." Father Lull said while turning the letter over, but not yet breaking the seal. Then he yelled, "JON!" while still staring at the unopened letter. A man about twenty years old appeared at the door. Jon was thin and short. He smiled at them all and said to Father Lull, "You bellowed?"

160

Father Lull said, "Please move the wagon that is out front into the stables and take care of the mules and horses. We will be out shortly to assist you. Do not bother the crate or anything else in the wagon."

Jon left to attend to the wagon and animals. Father Lull finally broke the seal on the letter and began to read.

Louis was eating greedily while William watched the father read the letter. William, being more concerned about the message's contents, ate nothing. After some time, Father Lull said, "Well, that answers some questions I had. I'll be right back. I want to send for Admiral Gregory. He will want to be here when we open the crate." Then, Father Lull suddenly left them.

William watched the retreating form of the Priest. Then he turned to Louis, who was more interested in eating than talking. "At least I know how to shut him up when I need to." William thought.

Soon, Father Lull returned and laid the letter on the table. He walked to the cabinet and, rummaging around, said, "Sir William, what happened to the others in your group?"

William relayed the story of their travels to Rennes-le-Chateau. The father stopped his search in the cabinets and turned to face William while he recounted the trip. William's voice grew sad as he relayed to Father Lull the part about them leaving behind Sergeant Bertrand, who appeared to be dying. There was a thoughtful pause after this. William, wishing the father would say something, finally prompted, "Father Lull, did the letter say what my party and I, such as what is left of us, are to do now that we have completed our task for the Grand Master?"

Father Lull said, "Yes. But I'm afraid your task is not yet complete. Have either of you had tea?"

Louis stopped chewing for an instant and looked at Father Lull and then at William. William, taken aback, said, "No, Father, but if I could know what we are to do now..."

Father Lull turned and reached into one of the cabinets, retrieved a ceramic container, and said, "We will discuss what you will do next, but to do that properly, I will need to share some information that has been kept secret for some time. The first of those secrets starts with tea."

Father Lull busied himself with preparing the tea as he spoke to them. "I am going to tell you of a great treasure that your

161

Templar predecessors brought out of the Holy Lands. It is the same treasure that your great-uncle, Peter de Sevrey, gave his life so that it could be spirited away out from under the noses of the Muslims at the Battle of Acre. There have been many rumors about what the great treasure is, but very few actually know."

Father Lull set one cup on the table in front of each of them and said, "This is tea; it is hot, so don't burn your tongue."

William and Louis both took a tentative sip, and Louis said, "Is that supposed to be drunk, or do we clean chain mail with it?"

Father Lull laughed loudly and said, "I didn't care for it much the first couple of times I had it either, but it grows on you. However, you'll probably not get the opportunity to drink it again. This may be all the tea there is in France, or any of the other countries you two are likely to visit next.

"Let me get on with my story. I'm anxious to open that crate you brought. This tea comes from China. I assume you've heard of China." Father Lull continued without waiting for a response, "It was brought by a Venetian trader who spent several years in the Far East. He is said to have spent a considerable amount of time with Kublai Khan, the ruler of the Mongols. On a few occasions during his travels, the trader met some of the Knights Templar, possibly even one of the Grand Masters, and a relationship developed between him and the Templar Order. At some point in his travels, he acquired some maps, which he gave to the Knights Templar for safekeeping. These maps are reputed to show parts of the world that Europeans have not yet discovered or know anything about. Some of the very small group of men who have seen these maps believe they are the work of imagination. Others in this select group believe they possess firsthand knowledge. It is these maps that the Grand Master has had you bring to me. Although I am not to hold on to them for long."

William sputtered, "Maps? We traveled all this way to deliver maps?"

Father Lull replied, "Yes. Not being a sailor or a trader, you may not understand the value of maps. There are many types of maps. Most of them are not accurate, nor are they meant to be. They are tools used to help illustrate to people who never travel further than they can walk in a day or two that the world is vast. But sailors and traders have maps that they keep to themselves; these

162

maps depict the real world as it actually exists. A good map that shows the way to established trading posts across vast stretches of open ocean or land is worth far more than a galley loaded with gold. These maps are far more valuable than one showing an established trade route; they show areas untouched by trade. These are new lands with new resources and new people. There is no way to put a value on such maps. If the information on these maps is what it is reputed to be and they are accurate, they would be of such great worth to a king and others that they might trade their soul to get their hands on them.

"And that brings us to the rest that we must discuss. On October 13, King Philip attempted to arrest all the members of the Templar Order and seize all their holdings. The raid was carried out quickly and successfully in northern France. In some regions, like ours, the arrests did not come off as expected. There were warnings that something like this was in the works. As a result, the Grand Master and some of the other highly placed leaders in the Templar Order took measures to reduce the impact an act such as this would have.

"Many of the ships were moved away from French ports. Some men have already been relocated to other locations outside the King's reach. Although King Philip tried to persuade other monarchs to make arrests, it seems he has not yet been very successful. He is presently pressuring the Pope to declare against the Templars clearly, but that has not happened...YET. I believe one way or another, King Philip will get what he wants, and the Pope will demand the arrest of all Templars everywhere. There are still some temporary safe locations for Templars. If we want the Order to survive, we need a haven to establish a base of operations and make a case to clear the Templar name."

William interrupted, "What exactly is it that the King is claiming we have done to justify such extreme measures?"

Father Lull said, "He claims knights are forced to deny Christ on your initiation into the Order and that the Order encourages homosexuality. There are charges of idolatry, heresy, and being secret tools of Islam; more recently, there have been rumors that some brothers have confessed to demon worship. Most are the same charges that were leveled against the Cathers and the Jews with great success not so long ago."

163

William said with less rage in his voice than he felt, "This is a mockery. No one would believe these charges."

"In that, you are wrong, my son," Father Lull replied, "People love to see those with power or status taken down. And the methods used to question your fellow Knights have provided many very damning confessions. There is little we can do about any of that at this time and from this location.

"Your group was sent just before the arrests took place. I am happy that at least you two and the crate have made it. I fear those of your party who returned to Paris are likely prisoners of the King. I'm sorry for the loss of the good Sergeant, but you two are still vital to the plans of the Grand Master to save the Order, regardless of what the King and the Holy Father decide to do."

Louis, finally having satisfied his hunger, said, "Father, it almost sounds as though you don't agree with the Pope, which I have never personally heard a priest hint at. Most priests I had the pleasure of meeting say every decree the Holy Father makes is from the lips of God Himself."

Father Lull thought for a minute and finally said, "There is disagreeing, and there is DISAGREEING. I'm concerned that the Pope's actions and reactions on this matter may have been made under duress and may not truly reflect the specific desires of His Holiness. I've always been a little outside the proper thinking of many of my peers in the Church, which is partly why I'm in Rennes-le-Chateau. I don't want to sermonize on this. However, there are aspects of the Church with which I do not necessarily agree. Although I understand the Pope is the head of God's Church here on Earth, I'm not entirely convinced he cannot be manipulated by evil men or even his own humanity.

"It seems to me all humanity is like a group of men in a boat with a slow leak at one end. The most powerful men sit furthest from the hole and rarely notice the leak's existence. The weakest sit in the leaky portion of the boat and try to shift their position in the boat away from the leak in any way they can. The powerful think that all the machinations of the men fighting and scrabbling to get closer to where they sit mean that those men honor and respect the powerful so much that they will do anything to be like them. And so, those in power feel they have a right to do whatever they think is best for the poor wretches they clearly don't understand. The

164

powerful assume the unfortunates are stupid and possess few redeemable skills. The least influential continually fight to stay above the rising water, threatening to drown them. The vast majority of those in the middle are shades of gray, varying between the two extremes depending on their proximity to the leak. Men in leadership develop an air of superiority so pervasive that they believe they are the only ones who know the truth and that the masses are incapable of understanding the realities of life. The powerful decide to make decisions for the masses and only tell them enough so that the unfortunate multitudes will do what the powerful want them to do.

"Don't get me wrong, I love the Holy Roman Church. However, I think the leadership has spent too much time in the dry portion of the boat and, to varying degrees, has lost sight of its true calling. I know this sounds arrogant on my part, and I fully recognize that I may be wrong…But I don't think so." Father Lull let out a hearty chuckle, taking the edge off his condemnation of the Church.

William, who was not entirely sure what the parable of the leaky boat really meant, was startled by the chuckle and unsure how to take it. On the other hand, Louis was smiling at the priest and seemed about to laugh when Father Lull decided to continue.

"Forgive me," he said. "I didn't mean to get so deep and philosophical. What I'm trying to say is that the power of Lords and Kings and even Popes tends to make them think that they know more than everyone else, and only their opinion counts. Many of the laws they pass and the decrees they pronounce promote that idea. And… well…I disagree, and I'm tired of it."

Suddenly, a man with a weather-worn face in an old riding cloak entered the room. His voice boomed as if he were used to raising it to yell commands: "Father Lull, why do you pull me away from my drinking and spreading lies in the tavern?"

Father Lull said in a cheery voice, "Ah, Admiral Gregory, I'm grateful you could tear yourself away. Let me introduce you to Sir William de Sevrey and his squire, Louis. Gentleman, this is Commander of the Vault of Acre, also known as Admiral Gregory, Commander of the Templar Fleet."

William stood and said, "I'm pleased to meet you, Admiral Gregory. Another knight pointed you out to me some months ago while you were meeting the Grand Master at the Commandery in Paris."

Gregory growled, "That damned fool. Won't listen to anyone. He bloody well better survive this so I can kick him in the arss and tell him, 'I told you so.' No offense to the damned fool intended."

William was somewhat shocked and didn't know how to respond. Father Lull clapped Gregory on the back and, with a laugh in his voice, said, "The good Admiral Gregory has a way with words, but trust me, Sir William Grand Master de Molay has no more ardent a supporter than Gregory here. I nearly had to physically restrain Admiral Gregory from assaulting Paris with his sailors to attempt to free the Grand Master."

Gregory said, "Enough of the pleasantries. What was I summoned here for? It's not time for dinner yet."

Father Lull said, "These gentlemen have brought us something you will want to see. Please follow me to the stables."

Gregory said, "Stables? I've seen a horse before; I have no damned use for them. Why are we going to the stables?" No one bothered to answer him as they all filed out to the wagon.

William and Louis climbed into the back of the wagon. William unlocked the lock to the chains, and they began to pry off the lid. Inside, they found several leather tubes, approximately three feet long and eight inches in diameter. The leather tubes had a thick coat of wax that completely sealed them. William took out the first tube and handed it to Father Lull. Admiral Gregory produced a small knife and began to cut through the wax around the caps of the containers.

"Is this what I think it is?" Gregory said, to no one in particular, as he worked the cap away from the tube.

Inside, he found a rolled sheet of thick vellum. As he began to unroll the sheet, he said, "God in Heaven, the damned fool did something right. I feared these were lost for good." Gregory looked at Louis, who was pulling more tubes out of the crate and handing them down to Father Lull. Gregory said, "Boy, how many tubes are there?"

Louis made a quick count and said, "Twelve."

"By God, they are all here, Father!" His face lit up with a smile that seemed very unaccustomed to the craggy feature.

166

Father Lull said, "I know you are excited, Admiral Gregory, but that will be enough blasphemy if you please." But he was also smiling broadly.

Confused and somewhat disappointed, William said, "Do these maps have anything to do with why the King and the Pope are attacking the Templars?"

Father Lull replied, "I doubt either knows anything about this map. To be clear, it's not 'maps.' These twelve sheets make up one large map. However, returning to your question, I am quite certain that the King of France is attacking the Templars purely out of greed. He wants their lands, and he wants out of the debt that he has accumulated with the Templars. The King also wants the money that the Templars have stashed all over France, or so he believes. I don't think the King likes having such a large, well-trained army in his country that he cannot control. With the Pope, it is more complicated. He may want some Holy relics your Order may have. The tithes that have been lost on all the lands the Templars have been given would be useful, I'm sure. But, I would say primarily, he wants someone to blame for the loss of the Holy Lands. It looks bad that so many popes who are supposed to be the mouthpiece of God have called for the Great Crusade and claimed it is God's Will. Then, for it to fail so completely…well, it might cause people to question the Pope's authority and infallibility. But, if the Templars are in collusion with Satan and they conspired with the Muslims, well then it's the Templar's fault, not the Pope's or God's."

William, still very much confused by all of this, said, "You told me maps are more important than I know, but I would like to understand why it was worth it for my group to have gone through all that we did to get them here."

"We will explain as best we can. Let us get these inside the church." Father Lull said. Then he turned to Jon, who was standing in a stall with a pitchfork watching silently, "Jon, we will need several boards brought into the church so that we can set up a very large table, approximately fifteen feet by twelve feet. Get a couple of carpenters to help you. Also, tell the cooks to prepare a feast of sorts; I think we will want to celebrate tonight."

Epilog

Late one night in the town of Clermont, a figure in a cloak was in the graveyard beside the local church. The figure walked with purpose to a fresh grave; the dirt was still mounded, and the tombstone had been recently set. The figure knelt before the headstone. He began to work by taking out a mallet and stone chisel, which he had borrowed from a stonemason. He carved a cross with four equal arms that flared out at each end. After completing the cross pattee, he carefully cut a circle around it.

The Priest, Father Patrick, heard the tapping of the chisel on stone and looked out through one of the transparent panels in the stained-glass window facing the graveyard. He noticed the figure and knew which grave the figure knelt before. Before turning away to return to bed, he made the sign of the cross and said quietly, "In nomine Patris, et Filii, et Spiritus Sancti."